FLIES

Sadie Smith

Flies

The Journal of Noreen Spink (née Purkiss)

BANTAM PRESS

LONDON · NEW YORK · TORONTO · SYDNEY · AUCKLAND

TRANSWORLD PUBLISHERS LTD
61–63 Uxbridge Road, London W5 5SA

TRANSWORLD PUBLISHERS (AUSTRALIA) PTY LTD
15–23 Helles Avenue, Moorebank, NSW 2170

TRANSWORLD PUBLISHERS (NZ) LTD
Cnr Moselle and Waipareira Aves,
Henderson, Auckland

Published 1990 by Bantam Press
a division of Transworld Publishers Ltd
Copyright © Sadie Smith 1990

Lines from 'Everyday' by Buddy Holly
reproduced by kind permission of Peer Music

British Library Cataloguing in Publication Data

Smith, Sadie
Flies
I. Title
823′.914 [F]

ISBN 0-593-02004-9

Typeset in 11/12 pt Mallard
by Colset Pte Ltd, Singapore
Printed and bound in Great Britain by
Biddles Ltd, Guildford and King's Lynn

For Craig,
bless him

People In It

Noreen Spink, née Purkiss, diarist. Overweight, very hardsome woman. Syntax is summing should be levied on courting couples, I think. I can't always spell right, either. Do me best

Stanley Spink, her husband, short, fat and balding. Youthful sexual bias confirmed years ago with arrival hotpants on the fashion scene, along with tall, soft-leather boots. A thigh man

Roderick McKay, Spink brother-in-law, a vigorous, black-bearded and eccentric Scot

Amy McKay, his wife, Noreen's slim and loving (and much younger) Sister. Religious

Dorelia Leech, beautiful Spink daughter and only surviving child

Wayne Leech, her husband, educationist and medallion man

Sharon, from the train shop, a cheap little whore

Larch Mulliner, a rich and predatory lesbian

Matron Peebles, a wicked old skinflint, yet withal a heroine

Big Mick, who swings both ways

The Family Elders, Aunts fat and thin, old dipso Uncle Eamonn and a horrible mother-in-law

Various workmates, barflies, geriatrics, policemen etc., also painted, Amstrad-playing dollies in employment agency and some ghosts

7

Note on MY LIFE
by Noreen Spink, née Purkiss

Dear Public

When I told him, Stan, that's my husband, I were writing this life of passionate, busty blonde (golden blonde now, I see to that; people have compared me to that Dolly Parton and she come off worst) approaching hem-hem years, he just looked at me all incredulous and said, 'We *know* someone like that? Get away . . .'

Unthinking, dozy prat.

So I shall write it straight, telling it like it is, letting it all hang out and revealing summing that would otherwise stay zipped up. And I shan't let *him* see it. I mean, I got a lot to say. About him, for starters and how he thinks he's demon lover, got *that which women'll kill for*. Well I know they all say that but do they all like it to be measured with a ruler? He does.

It's me of course the glamorous blonde from year of hemty ha-ha, same as Warren Beatty, Terry Wogan, that Jane Fonda. Oh and Donald Duck. It were a vintage year – even if I am putting on weight a little these days.

Free spirit, me. Passionate, like I said. Adventurous. Well, I would be . . . trouble is I got this milestone round me neck called Stan.

Still, I got £40 credit in mail order account and stripy little cat I love. Also beautiful, beautiful daughter and nice home.

But this ain't a Gumment White Paper, no. You just read on for all the rest.

Respectably
Noreen Spink, née Purkiss

Life just isn't worth living now my little girl has gone.

Even Miss Sweetbush on phone to say two new Aurora North-Brightleys in – now there's an assumed name if you like, I can always tell – don't help. (Also that Indira Candy back at last, about time, I had a card in for her ages. Also a Charlotte Lamb I haven't read.)

'But she was never here!' he cried. He sounded desperate.

'She *was*,' I said, dabbing at my eyes.

'Only for the last three weeks because of the Banns. Before that she was...'

'Don't go on!' I told him.

Annoyed, as any caring mother would have been, and he saw and shook out *Daily Mail* and hid behind it and lit up his pipe. Alright; we were in the lounge at the time, and it was Saturday.

'Cup of tea?' I asked and he said, 'If you like,' as usual, which drives me wild.

'You make it,' I told him and he drifted out, whistling *Balls to Mr Bangelstein*, most unrefined.

'Fancy a bit of a lay down presently?' he calls out all casual from the kitchen.

Do they ever stop?

Said to him in bed the other night we ought to be past all that sort of thing now and he just said, 'Eh? What sort of thing?' as he started in.

Can't tell him that for me now it's not like it used to be. He won't discuss things, least of all *that*. Beginning to feel like Auntie Vi. (Never been able to get much out of funerals.)

He come back with the Willow Pattern and five sweet-meal digestives, so lovely against my solid wood Welsh dresser with all the warmth of the mellow countryside beautifully crafted free feet to your door with solid wood handles and bun feet.

In my tiled kitchen (he did that) with Artex coved ceiling and artfully toning dildo knee-height round the wall you'd never know it wasn't real antique. Matches all my fitted cabinets.

'A real Olde Worlde kitchen,' Roderick remarked last week looking up at new plastic beams in breakfast alcove. 'Goes with the period garage.'

Don't care very much for that word 'period' in conversation.

'Tudor,' I told him. 'Elizabeth or James I.'

'James VI,' he come back, waggling his black beard.

Glad I didn't marry him. The curls of it get up your nostrils somehow. And there'd be a lot of that with Roderick.

I should know.

But Peggy Sue got married yesterday.

Baby was a vision in cream silk and yellow roses. Wanted her to have a crinoline but she goes for a Victorian look, all nipped-in waist with a bustle and skirts in front like those festoon blinds I got just lately for the bedroom.

She wore her dark hair up covered with little rosebuds – she gets that from Stanley's side – and the Reception was in that converted barn out Eden Park, the waiters ever so respectful. He said, 'We're paying. Bloody should.'

All in the street knew about it of course, I saw to that, though I didn't tell her next door. Her picture was in the local paper along with column mentioning Mother of the Bride. Wore my oyster colour three-piece mix 'n' match easycare, which I got Littlewoods M.O.

'I shall never get over it!' I was starting to say when

the back door went and it was Roderick and my dear Sister.

He was in fits over Plum's new milk bowl I got down Bromley Market outside on patio now because he slops the drips around and I can't keep clearing up. It has PUSSY written prettily all round it.

'Pussy?' Roderick laughs, pointing. 'Whose pussy goes in there for heaven's sake?'

Vulgar. Not having that in this beautiful Woolworth's school exercise book.

'Still over-feeding him?' he goes on. 'I'm going to call him Bellybags. He really should go on a diet.'

And my Stanley, seeing he's got company, joins in.

'The Steak 'n' Wine should do it, 'Reen,' he quips. 'Or the F-Plan. Or the Four Day Wonder. Mind you,' he said to the others, big silly grin all over his face, 'it's only called that because it's a wonder anyone can stick it for four days.'

More where this came from but won't be writing it. Men are so gross, except in Charlotte Lamb.

They all fell about, including my dear Sister who never has to diet, thin as a lathe she is, must have a quick metamorphosis or something.

'Ho, ho,' I said sourly. 'Works, though, dunnit?'

Bit of a silence.

'What I was going to suggest,' Roderick said at last, 'was that we all went up the pub.'

'No,' I said.

Didn't mind going for a drink. Well, I was still wearing my Aran doubleknit cardi (£39.99, BhS), my Prince of Wales check, mid-calf skirt and brown leather boots from shopping earlier in Bromley Mall, but I wasn't having talk about Baby's wedding in front of that black-haired Brian in The Feathers, the one there was all the trouble with before she married Wayne.

Secretly wonder if she hasn't inherited dark blood from me. Of course the Purkisses are Cockneys, everyone

11

knows that, but there's an Irish streak. Grandma Purkiss was an O'Kelleghan before she married and it's left some of us with a passion for dark hair. Well, men with it. Remember a time I thought I'd die if I didn't have a certain bloke might have been Brian's father.

Didn't though. Didn't die, either.

'I'm not coming if we're going to The Feathers,' I said now.

'The Black Swan, then,' Roderick said mildly. 'But smack it about, eh? Gasping.'

So refined. I just popped upstairs to give my hair a blast or two of (ozone-friendly) White Satin and tart a bit because I wanted to look nice. The Black Swan is a proper Inn, tapestry seats and old hunting prints, none of your spit-and-sawdust boozers. Shouldn't care for all those stone flags at home, though. You want to cover up that sort of thing.

Dora does ever such nice meals at the bar in baskets with red serviettes. He says puzzle her to serve Windsor soup, laughing a great deal at his own joke as always. Drives me wild.

He said now to Roderick, 'You can never just go with a woman around, can you? You think they're ready and you start out and then you have to wait, they're doing something.'

'Like check the window's shut and kettle's not switched on,' I said.

Went out through the gate into the alley. Stanley made a little door in it for Plum. I've had geraniums and trailing lobelias here all summer in pots on top of the wall which he painted to match. Not that she paints her wall next door, oh no but I like people to think when they get to ours *Somebody cares*. (Sometimes they say a bit more than that with aerosols and he has to paint it over but there's not a great deal of that in Kitchener Close.)

We got to the gate and I thought R. was going to start one of his indecent talks with the fishing Gnomes but what does he do but stumble over the caravan parked there as it always is and injure his big toe.

Should have thought he could have seen it. Big enough. 'Whoops! Mind the cara, Rodders,' Stanley said.

'Jesus,' Roderick muttered, and I said, 'Roderick!' because though we don't go to church, not since the accident, I won't have that kind of talk. Stanley knows. I saw him look at R. who was leaping around holding his foot. He'd gone all funny and white round the lips.

'You alright?' I asked, not wanting him to think I hadn't noticed. He didn't answer. He caught hold of Amy and we got out into the alley. Said I'd have my usual Cinzano and lemonade when we got to the pub. Roderick said he'd have a bucketful of Scotch.

Passed the end of next door. There was a FOR SALE notice tacked up on the breeze block and I thought That's funny, didn't use to be there. A bit of a shock. I mean, I don't speak, not after she told me P.G. Wodehouse was a good writer, but I don't like changes.

'Does she do Romance?' I asked, because I didn't want detective stories, however good, and I thought she'd got muddled with P.D. James.

'Oh certainly,' she replies, all innocence and ladida, though looking as if trying not to laugh. (Found out why when saw Miss Sweetbush later down the library.)

Well I tried a couple but couldn't get into them and told her so and she just raised her eyebrows and said persevere so I got back by calling our new kitten P.G. Wodehouse (sarcasm) who turned out to be a man making me feel silly which got shortened to Plum his nickname and putting out my washing earlier than her doing it overnight in my automatic using lo-rate, which wasn't hard as she don't get out of bed much before ten.

She just lies around all day eating wholemeal bread and reading. I don't think she ever shaves her legs. Not nice. And then I told her I and Stanley were having one of those surrealistic, log-effect, real-flame gas fires put in she sniffed and said personally she was all for natural substances herself.

Doesn't sound hygienic.

Lovely whiff of scampi up The Mucky Duck. I had two bags roasted peanuts, one of smoky bacon crisps, bit of his pork scratchings. (That too don't sound hygienic.)

'You could eat off of our kitchen floor,' he's fond of saying. 'If you like everything microwaved, that is.'

My dear Sister leaned across to ask what we were going to do with the other bedroom.

'Leave it like it is,' I told her.

'Mausoleum?' Roderick enquired.

'My house is my daughter's home and always will be,' I informed him.

'*Spinks' Nest*,' he said laughing.

'*Semper Idem*,' I corrected him. (Latin.)

It was educated Wayne who gave our home its proper title. I mean, time was when it was just plain No. 1. He'd been talking a great deal about ' 'Sixties Tat', by which he means pale brick houses with white gable ends and mock stone cladding on imitation chimney breast, just what we got. Then he suddenly thought he'd hurt our feelings so he came up with this dead classy name. Said it described the house exactly.

Well after that I got a name plate carved in wood, didn't I, down the timber yard where they do fancy stuff, and when I went along to collect it there it was all posh among the common lot; *Mon Abri*, *Dunroamin*, *Mapledurham*, and the rest – *Semper Idem*. Always the same.

(He'd wanted one of both our names together; *Reensta* or *Stananreen*, but I said no.)

Now he was on about having the bedroom for his trains, and I hit that one on the head as well.

'It's D.'s room and it stays that way,' I told him.

I've always looked down on those Northern women you see in telly sitcoms such a lot, figures of fun mostly,

14

but don't tell me there's smoke without fire. They bawl when they're sorting their men out. We're subtler here in the South. I often look at them and think You Poor Provincials.

No. I manage Stanley. I make him dance by skilful handling. And when I want something special I just keep on and on and the thing turns up for Christmas. Mind you, I do a lot of sighing in October.

The little devil shrivelled right up when I said no and almost shrank down in his pot of beer. Roderick smirked and Amy looked embarrassed. And well, I thought, not even half-rations for S. in bed tonight, if he's thinks he's going to put his engine in there.

I was annoyed he should have thought he could. I was incense, gold and myrrh. But I didn't shout because a bunch of ethnics came in just then past us. One of the women was especially striking, long skirts with a sort of bright bandeau round her head.

He came out of his pot and simply goggled. I could see his fantasy machine kick once then roar away.

Went home after that, I saw to it, and firmly past The Chocolate Box. Well, I was full up of nuts.

But we went into Readwell's because Amy wanted *The Good Christian* or something blah and there it was.

It had a little cardboard section all its own.

THE DEFINITIVE DIET BOOK!!! the headlines screamed at you. NUMBER ONE BEST SELLER IN THE U.S.!!! YOU'LL NEVER HAVE TO DIET AGAIN ONCE YOU'VE READ THIS!!!

Well of course I had to have it. So Stanley parted with four quid (it was a paperback), sighing, and it was mine. I'd give anything not to have to diet again.

On the corner he said Bugger it, he'd forgotten his tobacco so I said I'd get it and went back to The Chocolate Box for his ready rubbed and got a box of After Eight for myself and hid it under my chunky. Well, got to have something to eat while reading DON'T LOOK ROUND!!!

The men watched the sport while I got tea and then they went to the Offy for some cans for them and Nouveau for me and Amy. Later microwaved some pizzas out of the freezer and later still Roderick washed up.

Said thinking of getting a dishwasher soon, human hands didn't get things clean enough for me.

He said, 'What about the forks?' Told him I didn't know. If the machine didn't get them clean, Stanley could do them separately perhaps.

After they'd gone turned up the Magicoal, kicked off slippers and curled up with After Eights down a cushion and read DON'T LOOK ROUND!!! Did offer him one once but he was looking at telly and didn't answer so put it in my own mouth.

He very quiet. Glanced up once or twice and saw him breathing. So it just had to be a nudie show on screen.

Well it wasn't a beauty show, which he watches whenever they're on but it was a different one and no mistake, in Haiti or Singapore or China or somewhere else where they show their thighs.

'Cup of tea?' I asked him and he nodded, hardly moving. But when I came back from the kitchen the picture had changed and he was breathing normal. Well, normal for him.

I gave him his tea and he gave me a look. Knew then that he hadn't hardly recovered at all. He was sort of trembling and clutching the control.

Men.

Time was when he used to want me to dress up as a schoolgirl, and I did too even though I felt silly because of being (a bit) overweight. Still, we haven't had any of that for some time I'm happy to say.

But he was always keen. Affectionate.

'Going up,' I told him. 'Got a bit of a head.'

He nodded, the wild gleam fading slightly from his eyes.

I went up and washed as always and used French

16

Fern Mum and White Satin talc. I like to be dainty. Put on a clean wincyette nightie out of the airing cupboard, a thing which always gives me great pleasure, being nicely ironed and folded and smelling of fabric conditioner.

Popped my quilted hoousecoat on top, then creamed my face and put rollers in and then got into bed with DON'T LOOK ROUND!!! and a hottie.

I was just studying the boring exercise bit and nodding when heard him clumping about down below, locking up. Normally doesn't do that until I'm well asleep.

Oh no!

Heard him come upstairs and go in the bathroom and I lay there all cross and nervous. Why do men always pee gigantic like Niagra Falls? Then the bedroom door opened and he come in, all pink and obvious.

Knows I like him to wear pyjamas. Pretended to be asleep.

' 'Reen!' he whispered. ' 'Reen! You awake?'

I breathed even and loud. He got into bed. He snuggled close and I could feel him just lying there with it up, all hard and ready. Well, I wasn't going to move.

Come to think of it I should have turned my head and shown him a face all round and shining like the full moon and that would have put him off perhaps. But inspiration like that rarely occurs at the right time. I just lay still.

He pressed up tight and whispered, ' 'Reen!' again and groaned. I felt him fumble for a handkerchief, always keeps one under his pillow, and then he sighed good and long and his hold on me relaxed.

In the morning I found the handkerchief on the floor.

Well, thank God for my Super Electronic De Luxe Hotpoint, that's all I can say with three-speed tumble drier.

Had a bit of a lay-in this morning. Wayne always says that sounds like chicken protest.

He went for News and Screws because he hankers

17

after 'Nude Vicar in Bizarre Love-nest with Thirteen-year-old' sort of thing.

More thighs. I said, 'Makes a change.'

Ever such a lovely picture of Princess Di in colour book, nearly as beautiful as that Moira Stewart on TV, only not so posh.

Did sprouts and read some more of DON'T LOOK ROUND!!! They want you to give up beef.

Cooked an enormous roast (beef) with sprouts, peas, parsnips and really crisp potatoes, apple crumble and cream and thick, thick, *thick* custard. He moaned it was overcooked. Likes his with the blood running.

Tried an Australian saga Miss Sweetbush give me when Indira Candy a long time coming but couldn't get in. Who wants to read about the Outback?

And why so much Australian stuff on telly? Wayne says their soaps give new meaning to term 'Pommy-bashing'. Agree. So bland remind me of cottage cheese.

Well, they're only Poor Provincials once removed. Gimme EastEnders any day.

He saw me at the kitchen table and asked, 'What you writing in that book?' And I said, 'A trenchant modern blockbuster with veridical, international personages, near-catalysmic world events, obsessive homosexual love, espionage and incest; a potpourri of the Earth's great themes.' Well, I was reading it off of the book jacket on the table, wasn't I.

He said, 'Get away!' and stared.

Told him I thought of calling it GONE WITH THE WIND, and he said he was sure it had been done already.

Prat.

Later we were watching that middle-aged man and his holiday programme (he ought to cover up his legs) when he suddenly turned to me and said, 'Why don't you just call it BELLYACHE? You know, gone with the . . .'

18

Soon stopped laughing when he saw the look I gave
him. Drives me wild.

Watching all that sun and sand made me say 'You know,
I really fancy Tenerife this year,' and looked at him. And
that was when I first noticed the change in him. Yes, that
was when.

He didn't answer at first. Then he said, 'Well, how
about a little country cottage this year instead?'

'Here?' I asked, 'In England?'

'They do nice little flint places up on the Norfolk
coast,' he said. 'All log fires and videos.'

Reminded me of her and her natural substances.

I said, 'You won't get anyone these days without
video.'

'We on, then?' he asked quickly.

There was something funny in his face.

'Gimme map,' I said.

He went out to the car and fetched the AA book, and
I had a look and there was Norfolk like someone's backside sticking out into the cold North Sea.

'You're joking,' I told him. 'Winds straight from the
Urals. Noway. Tenerife.'

'But you'll moan about the flies again,' he said
weakly.

'Better have flies than send postcards from this country,' I told him. 'People would think we couldn't afford to
go abroad!'

He caught his breath and I looked at him. You can't be
married to someone for thirty years without knowing
when there's something different.

'Wouldn't mind,' he said, obstinate and rather
childish.

'Wouldn't mind?' I asked him. 'Wouldn't mind?'

And he subsided.

Feeling uneasy and I don't know why.

19

Got him off to work and then went down the High Street and registered with an employment agency. Haven't worked since me and Dorelia did tomato grading last summer.

(Could have gone to the Job Centre but you get all sorts down there. Might pick up something nasty.

And I didn't want a job washing up or charring for no ladida madams or anything, just a nice occupation for a coupla months to take my mind off things and make up for Dorelia's money not coming in. At least, that's what I told myself.)

A tarty piece sitting in there, playing a desktop computer keyboard. Looked divorced to me, you can always tell, they get very heavy-handed with the blusher. But there, I'm a tolerable woman. Besides, I wanted something.

She flashed her teeth and asked, 'Can I help you?' and I said I hoped so, I'd come about a job. Should have thought it was obvious.

'What kind of work-skills can you offer?' she asked, so I told about the tomato grading and being a dinner lady at Cranmer Road Infants' and about the home knitting and she asked could I type? Any VDU experience? And I said I had a CSE in Needlework and she hummed.

'I'll put you on our books,' she says. 'You'd accept office work, I take it?'

I said yes, because office work sounded ladylike.

'If it's a good, clean place,' I told her.

'They mostly are!' she says, pausing in her writing to shoot me a look.

Well she wrote down all particulars like age (took five years off as I was wearing plenty of lipstick) and she said 'Thank you so very much, Noreen,' almost as if I'd done *her* a favour. (Found out later what percentage commission she gets on each deal. I had.) 'Nothing right now, but sure to be something very soon, maybe tomorrow. Temps wanted all the time round here.'

She smiled again – great big white teeth she had like Royalty – and I went out into the street again, feeling chuffed.

The sun was shining and it was such a lovely autumn day went to get my hair done at 'Cut Above', you don't always have to book. This little pansy wanted me to have it really short and finger-dried but I didn't fancy his fingers so told him to blow-dry like I always have with just a touch of mousse or spray gel.

If I'd told him to spray it from his whanger he couldn't have been more shocked.

'But dear lady, that's out, right out. Positively archaic.'

'Rollers, then,' I said.

Well, that nearly finished him. He went off hurriedly for backup but I wasn't having no nancy-boy chorus telling me how to have my hair.

'We'll leave it, then,' I said loudly from my position in the middle of the floor. 'I'll go somewhere else where they know what they're doing.'

He whipped round and fluttered his hands at that and came back and whispered rollers were archaic too but I just stood there and looked at him and he muttered and flounced off and came back with a plastic basket full of them.

Well, he actually did it very nicely. But we didn't talk while he was working and I didn't put any money in his little box afterwards.

Then went and drew fifty from the joint and blew it all in Marks on a navy teryleen suit with permanent pleated skirt, little breast pockets (only I haven't exactly got little breasts) with mother-of-pearl buttons and a white Peter Pan collar.

Also tights, two slips, two bras, a little scarf and a blouse and a pot plant for the lounge. (Cheque)

But Size 18!

Bought three Mars Bars for a cheer-up and ate them in the Park.

21

Dressed up after tea.

'Bloody hell,' he said. 'How much that lot cost?'

Told him it was cheap – well, so it was compared with other things, like a suede coat. Then told about ELITE and he brightened up.

'You really got a job?' he asked and I said, 'Not yet, but I soon will have. Office work. That's why the suit.' And I went up and down the room, parading, so that he laughed.

But there's something on his mind. He opened his mouth to speak and shut it again and then went out of the room rather fast to play with his trains. God only knows what else he's got up there – girlie magazines I shouldn't wonder.

In bed before I was, waiting.

'All warm,' he says, meaning I suppose the bed.

'It's like bloody snow,' I said, climbing in. 'We really better get electric blanket.'

'You're electric enough for me,' he says.

Never no love.

Well yes, I know he is fond of me but he never says just then. Just when I need it things go all mechanical. Always have done. Two seizes of right titty, one quick one to left in case that feels left out (be more convenient if I just had one big one in the middle) a grab at down below and we have liftoff. Well, ignition.

So now he's twisting about in the bed and breathing, and presently he's stroking my legs. Then he heaves himself up and over, gasps with nice feelings and settles down to work, slow and steady but getting much quicker very soon.

And of course he is wearing his socks.

This is the way Baby was created all those years ago. Of course he gets quicker still, then there's a shout and the show's over, though not for me. And then of course he lays back, peels his mucky Durex off and drops it on the floor beside the bed.

22

And I'm left just beginning and thinking of Roderick, though that was over many years ago.

Those were the days, my friend.

And what we got now? Maybe I should see somebody. But who?

And what could I say?

Help, I been robbed. Somebody mugged away my proper feeling. Stanley's burps and 'Pardon me!' and laughing loudly at own jokes and wearing socks and being short and fat and common – yes, I got all those.

Who took away my feeling?

Stanley Spink and Time, the thieves.

They've stopped. Is it *that* or am I pregnant? Worried. A bit.

No good trying to ask the Countess here even if she did say (long ago) she wanted to be a mother to me. That's a laugh. Anyway I'd rather die than ask her about this one.

If only Mum was still alive.

Hoovering today when thought *can't* be pregnant. Cheered up. A bit.

Dusting and thinking how she's no right to the name Spink. I mean, we all play that she has all these years but she hasn't, things he's said from time to time.

He's got this secret fantasy his dad was a noble lord or something. I know.

But I ask you, who would want a mountain of lard with furry whiskers? Not a noble lord, you bet your last quid.

And if she's not Spink, then neither is he or I.

Well I got Purkiss to fall back on and Dorelia has Leech.

Made large fruit, a Mocha and a Victoria sponge.

Will start new diet tomorrow.

Kids back this evening, very brown, with washing. Theirs has had to go back with fault in the rinsing cycle. Made huge pot of tea and sliced up the cakes. Couldn't take my

23

eyes off of her, so slim and brown and pretty.

Not showing yet. Thank God she's married.

She said, did we get her postcards? I told her what postcards? Always the same with you. You post them on your last day stands to reason they'll arrive round Christmas.

She bending my ear about cervical cancer, elected women leaders and eating healthily. (Sounds if there was special way to put it in your mouth.)

She said men who not had little operation ought to carry Gumment health warning. Asked her if the matter should go before Parliament fairly soon. (Sarcasm)

And I think women owe as much to that Joan Collins as to that Margaret Thatcher.

Then she told me off about eating too much chocolate. Butter. Eggs. Cheese. Beer. Beef.

Stanley heard.

'Blimey, anything left you can eat?' he enquired. And when she told him said he didn't want all blasted peas and beans.

Wonder if that's what she's planning to feed Wayne?

'He'd been in Smith's on the way over. Two books.

'Ted Hughes,' he said, showing me.

'Well, I've heard of him but I can't read his stuff. I prefer Patience Strong myself or Helen Steiner-Rice. And not a thing I generally admit to, reading poetry. Wayne knows though because he caught me once, sending one of my little efforts off to *Woman's Weekly*.

He didn't give me his opinion straight away like I thought he might, him being an English teacher and all. I had to prompt him.

'You like it, then?' I asked. And he thought hard and after a bit said it was distinctly after the school of William McGonagall.

Chuffed.

These days I write mainly humorous verse.

* * *

24

'Though his eyes are small and piggy
My old man has got a biggy.'

That sort of thing. don't know quite what to do with it, though. There aren't many funny papers around.

Wayne's book fell open (the other one, not the Ted Hughes) and I had a look.

'They are not long, the days of wine and roses:
    Out of a misty dream
Our path emerges for a while, then closes
    Within a dream.'

Funny how someone else says what you're thinking. I mean, about Roderick and the old days. That was how things were and put so beautiful. Someone called Ernest Dowson.

Wayne looked at me and smiled.

'Some time these'll be the good old days,' he said.

You're joking. Wine and roses? Tea and sneezes.

Still, there was a time years ago me and Stan climbed a hill in Cudham down in Kent with a clump of fir trees at the top and sheep. Broken iron railing round the trees, everything very still, no one about, only sheep, blue sky and clouds white like the sheep, high up. Could have been anywhere.

Went over railing and he said, 'Do you want to?' (Affectionate even then). 'Don't say yes if you don't.' I said yes because I wanted to find out what all the fuss was about.

Dorelia would laugh if she knew. I mean, we didn't, not in those days, go 'all the way'. Usually me and Stan just stuck to heavy petting, which was an ugly name and very uncomfortable for the boy.

And I said yes too because I thought it would pay Roderick out. For choosing my dear Sister after I'd thrown him over.

Sauce.

25

Well, there was all cow parsley inside, and grass and first we sat and then we laid down and after a bit I took off my blouse. He kept his things on. He was skinny in them days.

He unhooked my bra. It was a Marks' one, conical, with points. Yardsa stitching round and round to give it fullness. Not that I needed it, even then.

I remember him just sort of gazing and saying, 'Oo-er!' over and over again.

I think it was the first time for him too. Well he said it was. When we lie down he didn't seem to know where to put it. Aimed and missed so to speak.

Anyway he managed it and it was all over very quickly. Remember coming down the hill afterwards thinking, 'That's *it?*' If I'da known I was going to get it now for thirty solid years I'd of waited.

I was still kicking myself too about sending that Dear John to Roderick, him off doing his National Service somewhere else down in Kent. He couldn't understand I had to have someone *around*. When he come back Amy was seventeen.

Would it have been different with him? Used to make me melt just holding his hand. I dunno. All I know is doing it ain't a bit like it's described in Mills and Boon.

A religious person in a mac came to the door today. Had papers and books to sell out of a shabby suitcase. Felt sorry for him at first as he started to hand out the good news before I properly realized.

Soon's I did I went to shut the door and he stopped his spiel right there and looked at me out of his watery little blue eyes.

'God's good, you know,' he said.

'Oh yes?' I said politely and nodded to show I'd heard. Time for a cup of tea and the digestives. And my new Queen Anne floral brushloom slipovers had just come White Arrow for the lounge and I was keen to try them.

And after that I planned to rearrange the hall. S. had put nails in and I was going to fix up those old bayonets of Grandad's in a cross and put plastic poppies round them. Oh, no doubt about it, I was up to here.

'Yes,' the little bloke said. His arms must have ached from carrying all that paper. 'And I'd just like to tell you . . .'

'Got statistics?' I enquired.

'No, but if you'd just give me two minutes of your time I could show you what the good hand of the Lord has done for me.'

That two minutes reminded me of Grandad's swords. I edged back from the door.

'And I could tell you what He's done for some others also.'

'Only some?' I asked. 'Choosy, is He, your God?'

Selective, like ELITE Employment Agency, he sounded. (Tarty little cow still hadn't rung.)

'What about all the cripples, then?' I asked. 'What about famines and earfquakes and floods? What about little kids born deaf and blind, and leukaemia and cancer and spastics, eh? You have a think and then you tell me if that's good.'

'I meant you personally,' he said.

'Oh,' I said. '*Personally* speaking, are we? Now I understand you. Personally then, if God's so good, why'd He let my little boy get killed? Why was there a drunk driver that day in Portland Road so he crashed into us and killed my baby boy? I've had to live with that for nearly thirty years. So you convince me now that shows a good and loving God and I'll go along with you and maybe buy your stuff. Until then – excuse me – I can't think it's anything but bad.'

Just looked at me and slowly shook his head.

'I can't tell you,' he said sadly. Stooped and got his gear together. He was bothered. 'I only wish I could. Good morning.'

27

I shut the door on him and leaned on it inside, listening to his footsteps going down the path. All the old, fierce pain was back and it broke like a wave inside me. I didn't bawl, but oh my little boy. My little, little boy.

After a bit I went back in the lounge. Fitted the loose covers, tidied up and put Suky on. Then I went up the shops.

Got three kinds of slimmer's soups, new book of calories, plastic belt with centimetres marked on it (there weren't any with inches) and a pair of size 14 jeans.

That Plum is a dear animal, always so clean and pleased to see you, lying on his back and giving little cries. Stoop and tickle his tum and he goes mad, rolling about all over the floor. Has six hard little pink nipples. I suppose you do get those on tom cats? Everything else hidden decently away under fur.

Roderick says for Pete's sake get him seen to. (Plum.)

Woke up screaming in the night. Dreamt the door-to-door evangelist came back with a message from the Queen to tell me exactly why little Darren had to die. Cried.

Then found he was awake, lying propped up on his elbow.

'Just a dream, Mog,' he was saying. 'A bad dream.'

He hasn't called me Mog for years and years.

Went downstairs and made a cup of tea and finished up the sponge.

Wondered how it would be if one day woke up and he wasn't there, all warm and hairy in the bed. Can't imagine.

He's got this idea of a country cottage fixed in what passes for his brain. Bangs on and on and on about it. Even says why don't we take the ten days owing to him?

I said, 'You're out of your tree. In November?'

He said, 'Why not?'

Well, I can't think why not, but people don't.

D. and W.'s honeymoon cards arrived at last, three weeks overdue like Indira Candy, saying loadsabananas, loadsacoconuts and living in shed you wouldn't keep your wellies in.

Puzzled. Thought they had booked into the Bridal Suite of local four-star hotel.

Gave into him in the end. Amy said she'd have Plum so I got a copy of *The Lady*. Wayne says you get a nicer class of oik in there.

He put the car in for a service and I sent off five letters with SAE to Norfolk addresses in *The Lady* which did holiday cottages to let. First one answers I shall phone to confirm and send off 10% deposit.

Wondered what to do if ELITE calls while I'm away. Amy says she'll pop in and explain.

Diet going well. Can get into jeans if I lie down flat on floor. Different story when I stand up, though.

Leaving tomorrow. Roderick and my dear Sister came round, wanting to go up The Swan. Jeans do up alright now but I'd packed all tops and had to rummage in a suitcase for them. R. asked if I was coming for a piss-up with the lads or was I going to stay here and ponce about in too-tight clothes?

No finesse.

Dora said Bon Voyage and watch out for the wind. Stan said got enough of that in bed, ho, ho.

Drives me wild.

Got here. Dartford Tunnel empty (for the Dartford Tunnel).

Titchy little place that smells of damp. You can hear the sea. But not at all, repeat not at all like Tenerife. Nor, for that matter, like South Norwood.

Bloody cold.

Sent off postcards this evening as an example to Dorelia.

Day Two
Narrow winding lane outside with flint cottages, two pubs and a little corner shop that smells of apples and detergent. Everything from cabbages to dog leads to the *TV Times*, which was nice to find.

But not a takeaway in sight.

He acting all rare and special. Saw why when I heard the trains. Don't mind them as much as I might. It takes you back hearing them whistle long distance over the flat fields. Reminds me of when I was a kiddie in the War. A happy time.

Day Three
He wanted to walk along the cliffs, brown up here. Didn't go much on the North Sea. Too cold and grey with waves breaking far out.

Saw a dead seal down on the beach but nothing you might call real entertainment value. Bloody cold.

Got busy washing everything in that kitchen, even the window. Stood and looked out. Nothing but a wild-looking marsh. Pulled the curtain even though it wasn't properly dark. Do miss orange street lights. And the gnomes.

Log fire in the living room and coke boiler in the kitchen. He got all sentimental, saying everyone had them in the old days. What beats me is anyone wanting them now.

Rarity value, he says.

You can stick it.

Lonely. Heard owls at night and with them and the trains it isn't quiet. But nobody to speak to. This place stands in its own acre of ground with trees and bushes. I said, ' 'S not natural, not having no neighbours to speak to.'

At least at home I have her and her novels. Well, I know I don't speak, but there's meaning in it. Here there's nobody to not speak to even if you wanted.

He disappointed I hadn't brought filmy nighties with me. Told him he had to be joking, I was frozen. Added he could keep Norfolk in November, which made him even more depressed.

Bought a stone pig in a junk shop in Cromer today. You unscrew the top and pour hot water in.

Two pigs in my bed—
Will it go to my head?
Screw and unscrew
Is what both of them do.

Wouldn't let him put his cold feet on it to warm up and he complained.

I'm sure it wasn't always like this, him making love to me as if I was another man. I know there was a time when we had a bit of gentleness first, and cuddling and laughing. We slipped into it naturally like, and I wanted it, I really did. In the old days.

Last night he grabbed my vital parts so rough it almost hurt. Even said, 'Come on, give us a bit.' In the end I just lay back and let him go ahead and played it was a smear test.

Last three days we been to one of the local pubs for our lunch. No microwave in the cottage of course, only electric stove with slot meter I thought contortionate. We'd already paid £10 deposit and that was more than the whole place was worth.

They did plaice and chips at the pub with little white

31

bread triangles, quite nice. He had brown ale and I wore my new jeans, although they were threatening to get tight again and burst.

On the third day he was going up for more brown ale and Cinzano when I heard a man's voice say, 'Heyup! Is it duck season before time?' – only he said 'dook' like awful Yorkshire Alf at home.

Landlord looked at me and Stan and grinned, not nice. Stan asked what was meant.

'Oh, you don't want to pay no attention to that,' says this publican. 'We get a lot of grockles in here, see? Stand all over the pavement cluttering it up and saying "Eh, duck, look at this. Reet champion."As if they didn't have no shops at all back home.'

'Oh, you mean *Provincials*,' I said, 'Well, we aren't ducks.'

'What part you from, then?' he asked.

'London,' I said. 'The South.'

'Oh, the Sarf!' he says, going into fits of laughter.

Suppose he thought he was taking off my accent.

Later other man came back again and I'm sure I heard 'Mutton dressed up as lamb' and 'Must be giving it away at her age.'

Shan't go in there again.

Tried to get Stanley to say something to the publican, but he wouldn't.

Wally.

Well, there wasn't much else to do and I got bored and told him so. Very flat, Norfolk. Rode on a little train to a religious place called Walsingham which is like Lourdes only we didn't have nothing to cure, only my sex life and couldn't ask Him about that because He's dead against all that sort of thing, isn't He?

Met three Men of God in a pub drinking whisky like it was going on ration tomorrow, which surprised me, but they turned out to be Catholics, which made it alright I

32

suppose not like those gloomy Methodists Amy took me along to once.

This was a laughing bunch and full of ideas for promoting the business, such as sky blue T-shirts with *Walsingham* on or blue and white candy floss and sticks of rock with letters BVM right through.

The third one said he had a holy relic – a finger of the hand of the builder who rejected the stone which became the headstone at the corner.

Don't know what our Amy would have made of that one.

Ate out in a pub overlooking the sea at a place called Sheringham and further along the coast saw 'Seal Trips' advertised. He said, laughing at own joke as always, how nice to take the poor things out on trips.

Drives me wild.

Miss the gnomes.

He said before we come away, 'Maybe we'll come up here when I retire. Take a cottage way out on the marsh at Morston.'

Over my dead body.

Really chuffed at being back. Hoover sounds like first day of the Somme. Sand.

Plum glad to see me, though not so much rolling about.

Asked Roderick if he'd been pining for me (Plum). Amy said she'd been busy (Plum again).

'How's this?' I asked. 'Busy? She?'

R. said, 'Eating well and all, but she's been out a lot. Couldn't keep her in. And smiling broadly when she did come back.'

Amy said, 'Hush, Roddy, that's not quite nice.'

Plum is a girl?

Well, put his shirts in at number 2 and down the library, tootsweet. Miss Sweetbush in there in dungarees looked up from long line of people she was stamping and said, 'Hush!'

33

Got large cat book in Reference Section with *Silence* notice up, and there it was, all about yowling and rolling and going out and being affectionate and so on.

Must have said something out loud because Miss Sweetbush looked over at me, put a finger on her lips and shook her head. Her monocle fell out.

Went home again and there was Plum lying on the front room hearthrug licking his nipples. Sat down and tried to think what this might mean.

'Hope you enjoy it more than I did, that's all,' I said to him at last and went to put his shirts out on the line. And then ELITE tart rang to say possible job for me on Wednesday.

Four days. I can get house straight and see Dorelia. And I can still get into the teryleen with the permanent skirt.

But still no sign of *them*. And sometimes I feel hot.

Be a saving on Tampax, though.

The worst, the very worst. Dorelia left Wayne.

Stanley said, 'Left him? Left him where?' – which didn't help.

Started with one of my feelings something wrong. Called their home. No answer. Went out into the street to get Plum in for his tea and there she was, hair all dishevelled, but that's the look now isn't it. Wish I could wear mine like that but we were taught to be tidy in my day. 'Groomed' was the word along with 'Poised'. Like Barbara Goalen.

Still, she looked so beautiful. Slim and still brown from lying in all that sun. But I knew something was up. Always do with her.

I said, 'Here's a fine thing. Where's your husband?' And she burst into tears right there in the street and said 'Mum, I've left him. I told him the baby was Brian's at The Feathers.'

'Oh you hussy!' I began, remembering all that fuss a

34

month before the wedding. Looked quickly round the block to see if the nets were twitching.

They were.

'Get inside,' I told her. 'I'll make a cup of tea.'

'*Is* it Brian's?' I asked when the door was shut behind us.

'*No!*' she wailed. 'I just told him that. He said I didn't do things round the house the way his mother did and I asked who made a balls-up of the hotel booking on St Lucia and one thing led to another and he's a plonker.'

'And you're a silly, silly girl,' I said, pushing her into the front room and that's when S. came in and asked her where she'd left him.

It seems Wayne buggered off. S. said he didn't blame him and I hit him.

Made a pot of tea.

In the end we packed her off to wait for Wayne at home. It's him she's got her explaining to do to. Hard, though. Wanted to keep her overnight. Funny how you never lose that instinct to protect them.

'You phone me when everything's alright again,' I told her, hoping to God it would be. 'And I'll come and see you.'

Sunday I couldn't lay in. Got up and cleaned. He went for his tits and bums. About nine the phone went and it was Wayne from Luton Airport.

'Your wife's at home,' I said, all cold. Well, he shouldn't have said that about his mother. 'I think she's waiting to talk to you.'

He said, 'Alright, Mrs Spink' (not Ma), and rang off.

All I can say is I hope this baby don't have blue-black hair.

They have this ducky little house up Anerley, end-of-terrace, ideal first home the agent called it. Wayne did the windows with that Norwegian stuff and put a cart-wheel painted white against the wall. She'd do well to hang on to him.

After dinner he got up and said he was going to 'SteamPast' his train shop on the roundabout at Elmers End, keeps open on a Sunday afternoon.

'Don't spend a fortune,' I reminded him. We've had rows on this one, 'cause he can go mad. He nodded.

He come back with four little wheels in a matchbox. Said he was going to build a carriage out of bits. Felt no end of a mean swine.

I watched *Songs of Praise* then got the tea and went to call him. He didn't hear so I climbed the ladder the better to shout and then I thought why not? Go all the way up and catch him reading girlie magazines with the business all in hand so to speak.

Stuck my head through the trapdoor. He was over at his bench making a little carriage like he said, a carboard thing with windows.

'Done it,' he called out when he saw my head. 'Made it for half – no, a third of the shop price. Come and have a look.'

'No,' I said sourly going down again. 'Your tea's on the table. Mind and don't let it get cold. Anyway, makes me giddy, climbing.'

Served me right, didn't it.

ELITE called again to say, What about Mulliner's?

I said, 'What about it?'

'It's big,' she said. 'Better money. They lease vehicles, all sizes, privately and out to firms in fleets. But they're also a mass of systems embracing conglomerates, domestic commodities, computerware and engineering. There's Mullinermainframes, Mullinermicros, Mulliner (euro)motors . . .'

'Don't go on,' I said. 'Just tell me how to get there.'

'Crystal Palace Parade,' she said, 'Job's in Vehicle Leasing.'

36

Pressed the teryleen and told S. about Mulliner's. He quite cheery.

Tuesday, call from D. to say alright.

He sitting up in bed this morning all dozy, but I couldn't stop. Usually if I've things to say to him I say them then. Sitting duck until he's got his trousers on.

But this morning said sharpish, 'Boiled eggs, that's all you're getting. I've got to get the bus.'

'Get your bloody own, is it?' he asked smiling.

(We were in this pub once and a couple came in and he went up to the bar with his mates and she hung around by the door. She said, 'Can I have a drink, then, Andy?' and he said, 'Get your bloody own,' and looked at his mates and they all laughed, men together.

Wasn't the laughter, it was the way he looked round at his mates.)

Caught the bus alright, nervous I wouldn't and got there early. There was a large car park and some swing doors and then a Reception area with lots of plants in tubs and ever such a fancy pink toilet. Powdered my nose.

At nine a girl come in couldn't have been older than my D. dressed to kill and I gave my name, saying from ELITE.

She took me upstairs to a large open-plan office with more plants drooping all dusty and dispirited and filing cabinets and desks. The air smelt dry as dry from the conditioner. Windows were blue. You couldn't see out of them, like *Dallas*.

A good-looking blonde with a hard face and thin eyebrows and no expression like Greta Garbo come up and said she was the office Supervisor. Showed me where to leave my coat and where to get a drink – there was all sorts in a dispensing machine in a corridor.

Then she give me a place at a very long desk set across

37

two smaller ones in a 'T', a pile of green invoices and said to me, 'Tick these off.'

You had to match the vehicle registration number to the same one in the ledger and then stick the invoice on a spike. If you couldn't find the number in the ledger you didn't impale the invoice but put it to one side.

'I'll show you later how to use the screen for missing ones,' says Garbo and went back to her desk on the far side of the room where she could watch everyone working.

Easy, thought I. But it wasn't very warm where I was put and some wintry rain and hail came lashing against the blue windows at this point. And the skirt suit looked too dressed up – several of the younger girls were wearing jeans. Still, I kept on at the job, thinking I'd be the best temp. Mulliner's ever had.

'Forty-five minutes for lunch,' Garbo had said. 'Most people eat at their desks so they're not late for the afternoon.'

I was wondering if there was somewhere to get a sandwich. Only had coffee before coming out because of butterflies. Looking round when two tarty bits came strolling up.

Sat down at other desks. Said, 'What you doing here?'

As they didn't look at me I didn't think I was meant. But one of them said it again, this time giving me a flicker of an eyelid.

'I'm a temp,' I said.

The two of them looked at each other and rolled their eyes up to the ceiling and then looked at each other again and sighed. Martyrs, both.

'Taking all sorts now,' one said and the other one giggled.

Meaning me? I wondered. No, they couldn't of. No one would be that rude straight off.

But yes, they did mean me, and they went right on saying things about me. They didn't want me at that T-shaped desk.

38

They thought they were there to chat, that was plain. They could do so easy while working, being so far away from Garbo. They got out books and pens, shifted their electric typewriters and started in.

'Lost anything over the weekend?' one asked when she'd finished saying she'd have to be dead before you caught her wearing teryleen. Her hair was heavily streaked in brassy lines. She had bad skin and plastered it thick with orange makeup. Chunky jewellery and ballerina skirts. Wendy, her name was and she never smiled. Mouth turned permanently down.

'Two grammes,' the other one replied. She was tall, nicely dressed, going grey, but what a face. Pauline, her name was. I nicknamed her Grouchy. 'Half a potato crisp for supper. You?'

'Nothing at all,' said Streaks. 'He came in and I said, "You want anything to eat?" And he said, "I'll get it myself. I know you're on a diet." "Well, please yourself," I told him.'

Thought suddenly of Stanley and the boiled eggs. At least I done him those. Still they give him a good lunch where he works, and an hour, not like here. All that French polishing makes him hungry.

Got up at this point. Well, I could bear to leave their conversation. Got a hot chocolate out of that machine and then seeing one for sweeties further down, got a Mars Bar and thought just for a moment things alright again. Then saw those two wrinkling up their noses and laughing.

They talked all morning, not saying much, just keeping contact, their hands moving over the machines all the time so it looked as if they were working. But they didn't say a word to me.

At first they talked in whispers, really rude, my mum would have said, but after a bit their voices grew louder as they got careless, treating me like the furniture.

'I told him straight, he can have it any time and I don't

39

mind what he does,' Streaks told Grouchy. ' "Anything reasonable," I said, "though not on Sunday. Don't expect *me* to join in all your little games without something back, though. I want something back," I mean, that's only right and proper, innit?'

She happened to look at me as she spoke and I smiled and nodded. She was furious.

'That how you got your Vitesse?' Grouchy asked her.

'And a ring,' Streaks said. 'And these.' She fingered her earrings. 'Well, I mean, fair's fair.'

But they really didn't want me there. Every time I got chocolate from the machine, they sniggered. Don't think it was particularly me they were against, any outsider would have spoiled their little club.

I put my Mars Bar and new copy of *Women's Weekly* with article called *How Not To Let Passion Become Obsession* where I could see it and promised myself a nice little read at lunchtime.

At twelve the whole room cleared off except me. Read my book and thought of money coming in. At one, all back and those two bitches went on laughing and whispering all through the long, long afternoon.

Home time at five. Thought Can't stand another day of this, will pack it in.

Went down to car park and there he was. So surprised to see car just stood still. Then I shouted and waved and those two bitches, who were right behind me, looked at him and sniggered loudly.

I didn't care. Put my head in the car window and gave him a kiss on the cheek. He wiped it away with the back of his hand.

'What you doing here?' I asked him, because he should have been just leaving, or beginning to drive home.

He looked unhappy. Face sagging in little grooves.

'Get in the car, 'Reen,' he said. 'Just get in the car.'

Got in and sat there. 'Well?' I said.

Nothing for some time. He just gripped the steering wheel and I sat waiting, with a sort of bubble growing bigger in my chest, a bubble of fear.

Suddenly couldn't bear it any longer.

'Baby!' I cried. 'Dorelia. Is she alright?'

'What?' he asked, making me want to hit him. 'No. It's not Dorelia.'

Sat back and breathed. I can take anything now, I thought, long as I know it's not her.

'Well?' I asked again, all calm and patient.

'It's me,' he said at last. 'Been put on half time. 'Reen. It's not the push, I'm not redundant – so they say. And I still got a full wage until January. But they're laying off another three hundred, streamlining the workforce here they call it, while creating extra jobs in Belgium. So that some who want to can go.'

'To Belgium?'

'EEC regulations coming in,' he said. 'And the plant here going over to kitchen units. We've all had notices.'

He always gives me things in little bits. I always have to make the picture for myself.

'They can't do this,' I said. 'Kitchen units?'

'They done it,' he said, starting up the engine. 'Next year I'll be mornings only. Unless we up sticks and go and live in Belgium or West Germany or somewhere.'

'Not b. likely,' I said, thinking of Dorelia and the baby coming. 'But the union. What's the union doing? You paid your sub.'

'Sweet FA' he said. 'They can't. Not even series of one-day strikes. It's this Gumment and the EEC Got a pistol to its head and it's legal. Wish we'd never joined or someone shoot the buggers.'

'Kitchen units,' I said. 'Made by hand, aren't they?'

'Not these,' he said, looking in the mirror and releasing hand brake. 'Going to have robots like the car industry.'

We turned out of the car park and joined the slow jam in the road. I thought some more.

'All a bit sudden, i'nt it?' I asked him.

'Not really,' he said casual.

'You known for some time, then?'

'Six weeks.'

'*Six weeks!*' I said. 'Six bloody, sodding weeks and you never even said?!'

'Never the right time to tell you,' he said. 'That's why I said take those ten days owing. I thought we'll get that in at least.'

'Oh, we should have gone to Tenerife!' I told him.

Thought of the Consolidated British Foods Shares my godmother left me ('Always money in bread and butter, 'Reeny dear.'). Also about our ones in Telecom. Wondered if we should sell them and invest. And there's the house. If you move north, it's cheaper.

Also thought about invoices and bitches and Christmas coming, and made plans to press my jeans.

'We'll survive,' I told him, though at that moment I rather doubted it. 'But not if I don't have summing to eat.'

'Oh yes,' he said, turning in our drive. 'Been meaning to ask you. Did you get on alright today?'

Shown how to use the screen today to check the reg. nos. It lets out a shriek if you balls it up and press the wrong tit. Everyone miles around know what you done. Entertainment for all.

Those two bitches had a field day while I was learning. Got the hang of it at last but they laughed like drains every time there was a shriek and there were plenty.

Wore my jeans today but that wasn't right either. They got a great deal out of those. The zip went halfway through morning. Uncomfortable inside and out.

Thinking about D.'s marriage and how we would cope if she became a single parent when another bloody silly little number went missing and had to go back to the screen. Felt really sick. Tried pressing the button very gently in case it could be fooled.

'Kick it,' a well-spoken voice advised. 'Violence is the only thing the little bastard understands.'

Astonished. First time anyone spoken friendly since I started.

A tall, very elegant girl with her hair in a bun was watching me. Very laughy brown eyes. Couldn't see whether she was wearing makeup or not, but she looked good. Style.

'Or pull the goddamn plug,' she said. 'But that might send the entire system down and God knows it doesn't need an excuse. Stick to blows and verbal vitriol, if I were you.'

She smiled and walked on across the room. I looked back at the machine. Very tempted to kick it like she said. Pressed keys hopefully and lo! A list of numbers sprang to view.

Still cheerful as I went back to my desk. But then I saw my neat pile of alphabetically arranged invoices scattered all over the floor. Bent down to get them – and Grouchy's high heels came quickly, dangerously near my hand. Nearly lost it.

Rearranged invoices and put them in pile on top of the open ledger with a stapler, an ink pad and a Mulliner Vehicle Leasing stamp to hold them down. Went to get chocolate from the machine.

When I came back, put the chocolate in its little paper cup down on the ink pad for a second because thought I could hear heavy rain on the roof. Went over to nearest blue window. Saw this section of the roof was flat and there were workmen up there, apparently doing repairs.

Went back to desk.

And while I'd been gone just that little minute someone had upset the chocolate. The hot mess was lying in a pool over the open pages of the ledger and most of the printout with those close green lines that give you migrain if you look at them too long were all mushed up and blurred. You just couldn't see the numbers any more.

I lifted the dripping things off the ledger. The invoices weren't too bad. Held them over metal w.p.b. and then looked at Grouchy and Streaks. They were typing as if their lives depended on it and for once they weren't talking.

Poured most of the chocolate off the ledger then went across to Garbo with it, dripping all the way. Don't think the bitches expected me to trip to Garbo. Typing stopped.

'I'm very sorry,' I said and held out the ledger. 'I've . . .'

'Don't matter,' she said, almost refectorily and smiled and I suddenly saw there hadn't been anything personal in the cool way she'd spoken up till now. She was nice. 'It was last year's. That's why you had to chase so many numbers. Take it to Bob' – she pointed with her biro – 'And he'll give you this year's if he's finished with it.'

I went across to Bob and he was nice too.

Well, there was quiet after that on the Western Front for a bit and I kept my head down and got on. About eleven thirty I went to the Ladies and there was the friendly tall girl with the eyes.

She was tucking wisps of her long hair up in the bun.

'Hi!' she says. 'I'm Larch. Who are you?'

'Noreen,' I said, wishing to God it had been Anya or Elspeth or Victorine.

'Like the outfit,' she says, smiling. 'Been here long?'

'I'm temping,' I told her and she looked pleased and said 'Welcome aboard.'

Struck me as a funny thing to say.

For lunch I'd brought sandwiches and *Woman's Own* and for a fleeting moment wondered if I should ask her to sit with me. But she just smiled and left, and I went back.

44

About four got up to get another chocolate and yes, you'd have thought I'd have had enough sense not to leave it on the desk again. Maybe I thought lightning wouldn't strike in the same place. At any rate I had to go up to the screen again and when I got back the little paper cup was on its side and there was hot chocolate streaming all over this year's ledger too.

My heart sank. I thought This is it. I'll get the push now and ELITE will be told and I shan't get another job. Ready to cry, thinking of Stanley and half time. If I'd thought of little Darren at this point I should have.

Didn't.

'Which one of you two bitches did that?' I asked in a loud voice. 'Or did it take two of you to spill my cocoa?'

They didn't answer. Sort of smirked silently. And then . . .

. . . our Larch came over. Looked at those two and they quailed. No other word for it, they quailed alright.

'How very peculiar, Noreen,' she says, righting the paper cup. 'That's the second time today. Either you're very careless or these cups are most unstable. If it should happen again, let me know at once, will you?'

She walks off and for the first time those two turned to me. God, they'd gone pale.

'Satisfied?' Grouchy asked.

Shrugged. 'You did it,' I told her. 'You been rotten ever since I come in.'

Then I thought I might as well rub it in.

'That Larch saw. She must have been watching,' I said.

Was about to add 'And she'll probably tell Garbo,' when realized I didn't know Garbo's real name.

'I suppose you know who she is?' Streaks asked.

'No.'

'That's Larch *Mulliner*,' she said, and waited to see what effect that would have on me. When I didn't

45

immediately gasp and fall fainting, Grouchy added 'Old Mulliner's granddaughter.'

Had a bit of a think.

'What's she doing here, then?' I asked. 'I mean, surely she doesn't need . . .'

'Haven't you heard of Creative Management?' Streaks asked all contemptible. 'Floor experience. She's got to know it all.'

Shrugged again. Couldn't think what to say except I was glad.

They gave me up after that and turned back to their typewriters again and really did some work for a change. There was no more persecution. Don't think I ever spoke to either of them again.

He was there again in the car park at five.

'Save your legs,' he said, pushing open the door. 'And the bus fare,' he added, gallant as usual.

'Just drive your car,' I told him, getting in.

Larch has moved me away from the draughty area to a spot with a radiator and a window I can open. Fresh air if I want it and not cold.

No jeans today. *She* wears designer clothes.

Telephone with little squares on my desk. Garbo said forget invoices, told me to take calls – queries, reservations, etc., which I take down and feed into a keyboard (not the Shrieker). Getting quite fast and can say, 'Mulliner Vehicle *Leasing*' in a posh voice on the phone.

Wore my navy linen-look twopiece today with white piping and matching belt, also blue slingbacks and white Orlon cardi. Sprayed my hair heavily with White Satin before I come out and then fluffed it up like Dorelia.

Larch in office again today. Came over and asked, 'How's things?'

I really enjoy my telephone voice and make sure most

people near me do too. It's not unlike hers.

Larch in again. This time she said, 'Look, we must have a drink. What are you doing lunchtime?'

Everyone in office listening. Kicked *Woman and Home* with article on Chocoholicism a little further under desk and smiled brightly up at her.

All changed in here. Atmospherics are completely different now. People on other side of room look across and wave. Garbo can't explain work fast enough. Even the two bitches tried to say hello.

We went out to this lovely little pub at Beckenham, all corner nooks and soft piped music.

'Have a Barley Wine,' Larch says.

'I got to work,' I said, shaking my head. Did she think I was stupid, out with the Boss' granddaughter? But she bought me one all the same.

'Got to be back by one,' I told her and she said, 'Relax!'

Her saying that reminded me of the one about the loony doctor had a skinful and screamed WILL YOU RELAX!!! at patients and then was relaxed himself, all over the floor.

She laughed heartily.

She is fun to be with. I never had a friend like her before.

Back well after two. Garbo didn't even look up.

Larch has a sports car, a Gilbern, enters it for rallies and so forth. Also she hunts, down in Kent. Asked me if I did.

And here's Friday, everyone still nice as nice.

And a pay packet.

Saturday

D. and W. away tonight, visiting his (perfect) mother up in Colchester.

Friday evening Roderick and my dear sister came

round with two old films and one of those boxes of wine. Bored. Sat through Charles Dance film dreaming of wine and roses. Bet *she* never had a Stanley in her life.

Thinking back. The more he had the more he wanted in the old days. After that time up the hill in Kent with the sheep he took to making special trips across from the workshop to Costing (Bainbridge's) where I was counting ten shilling notes. Used to use the connecting glass and steel bridge intended for Management, cheeky sod. He always kept his brown overall on.

Used to arrange to meet under cover of inspecting heating. (*That* didn't last.) Hadn't got a car in those days, only an old pushbike and both living with our Mums so it was difficult. Used to go to the pictures Friday and sit in back row of the Stalls, 1/9, Gaumont in Lee High Road.

Better still we'd sit in his front room and listen to Buddy Holly. I love Buddy Holly. Used to annoy me the way the Countess used to put her head round the door all wet and plastered down, covered with little rounds of pin-curls. Friday night was Amami night.

'Ev'ry day it's a getting closer,
Goin' faster than a roller coaster . . .'

Yes, that was our wedding day. And I couldn't really think why I was marrying him except that everybody did, you'd got to marry someone and I should wear a ring. Also I'd score off Roderick who by this time was interested in Amy and refused to listen when I tried to tell him I hadn't really meant what I'd said in the Dear John.

But of course all Stanley wanted to do was snog.

I used to wash my hair and put clean knickers on before I went over to his place in the evenings, but I might just as well have not bothered.

'Get 'em off!' was all his cry.

And then of course when the Countess (only she wasn't

the Countess then) put her wet head round the door who had the frantic scramble to look all unconcerned and decent? Not Stanley Spink.

I used to kick my bra under the settee. Puts you off nooky for life.

Nice girls didn't then, not even with Tampax, as I once heard in a Health Lecture we was give at school. Remember wondering how you could with Tampax, and still do. I mean, *thin*. Never could have tried it herself that lecturer. You want a Victoria plum for that. Didn't put up my hand and tell her, though.

All rather high on British Wine this evening. It wasn't very nice, but alright with chips he went out and got. They went about eleven.

That Amy has got Religion badly. Always had in a small way, joining first the Congo then the Presbo because of Roderick and of course it's the URC now. Also she's been buying books – only paperbacks, not too costly, but it's the thin end of the wedge if you ask me. Amy's out of proportion.

Went round there Sat. morning (bit of a head) because she often does me jacket potato and salad with garlic and curd cheese before I go on to Dorelia's. Will say she's amazing with food, my dear Sister, in spite of not having had children. (Why not? Would dearly like to know but she'll never say.)

Losing weight again. Well it's easy when you're up against designer clothes. Waltzled in to tell her not too much curd cheese and got small shock.

She knew about Stanley and the half time.

They'd met up the shops and he'd told her. Oh, everyone talks to Amy.

'You were buying trains together I assume?' I said.

'Oh, I don't think he was actually buying anything,' she replied before she could stop herself and then bit her lip. Saw Roderick frown and shake his head and

49

wondered why. Felt suddenly as if the ground had shifted ever so slightly under my feet.

With another woman you might think saying that was just plain bitchy, but not our Amy. She simply doesn't think.

'Anyway, we're both praying for him to get another job,' she said, turning away to the cooker and the potatoes.

I said, 'Thanks very much, that ought to put the mockers on it nicely.' Not because I was ungrateful but because I thought her praying was sod all use. I mean, God doesn't hear. Or if He does he doesn't bloody listen.

Well, you'd have thought after that she'd have left well alone, but no. After the potatoes she talked about little Darren.

'God saw you through that,' she said, as if it was all over.

I was so furious I hit her.

She sat there for a moment and then got up and left the room. Well, she had a lot of that from me as a child.

I was left with Roderick.

Think he was angry. His big Scotch beard bristling all over. Very controlled, but angry. I could tell.

'The trouble with you,' he began. Then he stopped and started again.

'The trouble with you is you won't let yourself get over things. You've never learned to bend with the wind, have you? You've never said to yourself, "Right, that's it. I can't change things, so I have to accept them."'

'I haven't got to accept it!' I told him. 'I don't have to accept anything I don't want!'

'Bloody have, you know,' he said, a bit quieter. Then he added 'And I'll tell you another thing since we're talking. *You're jealous* because Amy's smarter than you are.'

'I am not!' I shouted.

'And slimmer,' he said, piling it on. '*Kinder. That's one*

50

of the reasons why I married her instead of you.'

'O-o-o-oh!' I said. '*Liar!* I wouldn't have had you if you'd gone on your bended knees.'

'It was you who was on bended knees,' he pointed out.

Well. I wasn't standing for that. I left the house. Didn't even stop to put my potato skins in the swing bin. Damn them. Amy and her religion and her husband make me *sick.*

Nearly in Ds road before thought he told me once they squirt chilly juice in elephants' eyes so they smart and they don't feel claw marks when taken on a tiger hunt. Was that what he was doing, distracting me so it didn't hurt so much, thinking about little Darren?

Anyway, Amy isn't smarter than me. Or kinder.

Slimmer, maybe, but that's as far as it goes.

Was coming up the corner of Dorelia's road and there was this voice.

'Now, Baby dear, what have I told you? Surely I taught you better than that. First the shirts, then the panties – don't mix the sexes – and then all the little socks together in a row.'

'But, Mummy,' came Dorelia's voice, 'all the little socks will go off in ones and get divorced.'

'Then you must peg them in twos, Baby dear. I have told you and told you, a washing line must be orderly. Whatever will the neighbours think if they see vests all hanging up with the tea towels?'

Monkeys, taking the mickey like that. Popped my head up over the fence and that shook them. Dorelia and her Wayne were standing by their rotary clothes line.

'Ah, Mother-in-law, arising like Pluto from the bowels of the earth!' Wayne said.

'If I'm Pluto, you're Mickey Mouse,' I told him, going round to the gate. 'Going to ask me in or have I got to stand here all day like a box of eggs?'

(I never go in unless I'm asked. You hear of these fond

mamas, charge in soon as their kids are married and demand a key, but not this person. Besides, Wayne wouldn't give me a key even if I wanted one.)

Went up and took the peg bag out of Ds hand.

'Gimme that. I'd better do it,' I said.

'Dorelia can cope alright,' Wayne said. 'Just needs time to think the operation out, which pegs for which clothes and so on. Let her try. You'll see.'

'Oh, go and put the kettle on,' Dorelia said.

When we come in after pegging the washing there was a tray all nicely laid out with sugar in a bowl and biscuits arranged in a flower pattern on a plate. Stanley couldn't have managed that in a million years.

'Oh, I'm one of the New Men,' Wayne said when I looked.

'?' I said.

'Oh, the sort that let their wives go out to work while they stay at home being clever with the Hoover.'

'You don't mean Dad, I hope,' I said, dunking a Bourbon biscuit in my tea and forgetting they didn't know about Stan.

'Lord, no,' he said. 'He can't use a Hoover.'

'How's teaching?' I asked, to change the subject.

'So-so,' he answered, looking bored. 'Too many effing kids and too much bloody paperwork, but it's a living.'

Didn't like the tone of that but let it go.

A removal van parked outside next door when I got home. Talk about crates of books. She won't find it easy to get into P.G.W. tonight. Didn't say goodbye.

Larch not in office this week but everyone still very friendly.

Bought two new outfits, ever so efficient and tasteful in red and cerise, and a pair of green, wrinkled ankle boots. So we end up in the workus?

Still losing weight.

One funny, funny, *funny* thing today. The workmen up

52

mending the roof drilled too hard and one fell through right on to Grouchy and her desk. She screamed! Plaster everywhere!!

Wonder his and her necks weren't broken. Laugh? I very nearly died. She was all white plaster from head to foot and so shaken she had to have the Nurse. Not much whispering and swapping diet notes today.

Christmas Shopping

So busy have hardly had time to write. D. said wanted more baby things but I say you should have something pretty for yourself when expecting.

Got her some Janet Reger lingery. Said to Stan, 'That'll please Wayne.'

He said, not looking up from his *Mail*, 'He's already been pleased.'

Yes, well.

Half day Wed. for Christmas shopping.

Called Amy. Said I was sorry I hit her. Told her to meet me Mulliner car park, two o'clock sharp.

Got a weakness for Sevenoaks and little bun shop there. Place like one me and Mum used to go to in the old days. Told her so.

''Course, I was only child until you come along,' I said.

'Don't let's quarrel today,' she replied.

Who's quarrelling? Just stating fact.

Got a train Penge East, only ten stops down the line. Laughing and kidding about. Really did begin to feel festive.

It was an overcast afternoon and the lights were on in houses. Most had decorations up. I like to see in, especially at Christmas.

'Got a tree yet?' she asked, and I said, 'Too right.'

(Had started to put things on it but caught Plum looking at her reflection and then smacking the baubles for

53

all she's worth. Know the feeling. Have same impulse to smash mirrors Monday mornings.)

Went through Petts Wood.

Amy said, 'National Truss. Wouldn't half like to live there.'

Told her to forget it. The Purkisses have always been Londoners, esp. Dad, who was a real square-mile Cockney.

Had tea early, well, just egg on toast and pot of tea for two, but really enjoyed it. Then went up High Street where they got mini-market. (Not the livestock one down by station but up towards Knole.)

Feeling really chuffed and Christmassy. And then, of course, things started.

Had bought loadsa cheap wrapping paper, gardening gloves for Wayne half price, and model trains album for Stanley. Then made Amy go away while I got her new knitting bag and when she come back her face was all crumpled and she looked upset.

'Wassup?' I asked her and she pulled my sleeve, the way she used to do when she was small.

'Look over there!' she whispered. 'Oh, I can't bear it.'

Back a bit from the other stalls was one selling animal foodstuffs and brickabrack, fancy studded dog leads and so on, with man in black whiskers and flat 'at in charge. And by the side of the stall, tied up too tightly with a piece of string, was a small dog. He couldn't sit and he couldn't lie but kept shifting his position all miserable, and craning his neck at every passer-by and whining. Perhaps he thought they'd help him. No one did.

Time to time he'd put a front paw up to his face and rub it and whimper to himself and I soon saw why. He'd been muzzled something cruel and there were thin, tight straps cutting into his nose.

He wasn't a puppy, but he wasn't very old and still, when he wasn't rubbing his poor face, full of that eagerness they have, straining at things, and feet. He was getting shoved about a good bit, not because people meant to be unkind but because he was in the way there, and couldn't move.

Well, I made a show of holding Amy back, but I knew it wouldn't be no use. She thrust her parcels into my arms and started forward.

Flat 'At didn't want to know. Kept saying, 'Not for sale,' not looking at her, seeing to customers and obviously thinking she'd go away. Even bent down and pulled the little beast's string tighter so it yelped.

Amy said nothing, but moved away round the back of the stall so she came up with me again and asked me for nail scissors. Lucky I got some in me bag. Then she went round the back of the stall again, snipped the dog's string and tried to lead him away, all the while Flat 'At was dealing with giving change.

Well the dog couldn't walk, or it wouldn't, not at first, so Amy has to scoop it up in her arms. That's when it whined, looking back over her shoulder at the man. Some people don't know good luck when it hits them.

Quick as anything Amy dived into the crowd.

'Oh my God,' I said, following her with my eyes. Don't think many around realized what was happening, they was all too busy with their Christmas things.

When the top of her head disappeared I went after her. She was making for the London Road, damn fool thing to be doing, first place he'd look. Glanced back – he'd seen the dog gone and was shouting and waving to someone to come and look after the stall. Couldn't leave it till he got them, which gave us a chance.

Didn't like to run in case I looked guilty, besides, I had all the parcels. But after a while I caught up with our Amy in an alley that led into Buckhurst car park where there's a swimming pool and a library.

It was dark in the alley. She bent down and snipped at the muzzle.

'Careful,' I said. 'He might bite.'

55

But he never. He whined and looked up at Amy and licked her hand and rubbed his face with a paw and then stood about as if to say, 'Now what?'

That's when I knew she done the right thing.

He could stand and he could walk, which was a relief. Half thought he mighta been crippled, the way that man was treating him.

'Can't stay here,' I told her, looking all about. 'What you going to do with him?'

'Take him home.'

'You can't do that.'

'Can't I?' she says, very Purkiss all of a sudden. You got to hand it to Amy sometimes. 'What would you do, leave him here?'

'Don't be daft.' Didn't know what I had in mind, some idea of taking him down the nick or something. But the nick was miles away. 'You going to keep him, then?'

Silly question.

'You go and phone Roderick,' she told me. 'If you can't get him, get Stan. One of them must drive us home.'

'Oh, they'll love that,' I said.

'What are husbands for?' she asks, more Purkiss than ever and I stared at her. You think you know Amy and then you don't. 'Go on!' she says. 'Don't stand there. Me and Fella here going to hide out behind the cars.'

'First place they'll come looking,' I said, but I went to phone.

I got Stan.

'Sounds like theft to me, pinching someone's dog,' he said, being a great one always for the obvious. He sighed. 'Be about forty-five minutes, probably over an hour with all the seasonal traffic.'

'We can't stay hid that long,' I started to say, but he had sighed again and rung off.

Went slowly back to Amy. Began to be terrified she might make me take the dog in the Ladies for a drink. And

56

I was dead nervous of that stallholder. He was bound to find us.

The little dog widdled against the hubcap of a Ford and I said, 'You common thing. Should have picked a Rover.'

Well, there were plenty of them about, it being Sevenoaks.

It got very cold and dark, even with the light from buildings around. The car park began to empty and we had to keep shifting about, staying in shadow. Don't know what the dog thought we were up to.

The stallholder never showed.

At last Stan come and we pushed Amy and the dog in the back and shoved their heads down and drove out of that place. Shan't go back to Sevenoaks this century.

Roderick at home and dint say much, though he listened. Then he got out the Glenlivet and looked at the dog's cut face and I thought it might be in for some malt whisky, but no. It got a pail of water and some steak and kidney from the frig. and R. said, 'What a swine,' and squatted down to watch him eat, meaning the stall man.

You never saw food go so fast, except maybe Stanley with liver and fried onions.

'What you going to do with him?' Stan asked, and funny, we all looked at Amy. 'Shouldn't think there's much danger of him being traced, but if I was you I'd paint his little shirt-front out. That's what 'orse thieves done in olden days. I read about that in a book.'

'Never mind olden days,' I said. 'What if he licks it off and poisons hisself? Look at him now licking.'

'You'll have to call him Wanky, Rodders,' S. said, watching.

Well we pushed off after that.

He said in the car, 'You got to hand it to Amy, you know. She's smart and kind. Fancy rescuing a dog like that.'

Would have crowned him only he was driving.

*   *   *

57

Elastic in all his Y-fronts gone so in lunch hour got him 6 pairs of boxer shorts in Bentall's and because it's nearly Christmas some in holly pattern, some with Father Christmas and some with little red crackers on.

Also they have BIG BOY on the washing instructions label.

Said, 'I can't wear these things!'

I said, 'Ashamed of telling lies about ourself are we?'

'No!' he said. 'I mean, it's not a lie.'

'You got a little red cracker in there, you should have them on your pants,' I told him.

'Not so much of the little,' he said, going smirk, smirk, smirk.

'And you're always telling me Father Christmas is coming,' I added.

'Oh, he's coming right enough,' he said, laughing at his own joke.

Drives me wild. But we didn't have no more grousing.

Boxer shorts should give it all an airing.

Auntie Florrie and Auntie Vi coming Christmas Day and sleeping, also the Countess (yuk) and Amy and Roderick. With Dorelia and Wayne, as Stanley said, there'll be four more women than men. I said we could always ask Miss Sweetbush from the library to even up.

Stanley doesn't think much of Miss Sweetbush. Says he can always smell cherroots on her. He likes them fluffy like her in the train shop. Well he's not having *that* gift-wrapped and all done up for Christmas, that much is fixed and certain and for sure.

Idly drawing doodles on desktop at four today when Larch Mulliner blew in. Garbo sat up all smiles and bright attention but she satcheted over to me. Sadly, phone hadn't rung for hours, so she couldn't hear my telephone voice.

Still, she didn't seem in the mood to notice things like that.

'Ready to go?' she asks.

Was I? I was. We swept out past Garbo, Lady Muck throwing out something like taking Noreen from you, and down to the car park where she stopped for the first time to get her breath.

'Anything up?' I asked, casually, to show I was discreet.

'No, no,' she said. 'It's just that minions irritate at times.'

Couldn't think of a reply to that one.

'Let's go, then,' she said, brightening. 'I could use a drink.'

We piled in the Gilbern and roared off. In the vanity mirror I could see the vague shapes of heads all crowded to the blue windows to see us go.

I was sure we'd be picked up, the way she was driving. We got on to the M25 in ten minutes. Prayed it wasn't Sevenoaks she had in mind.

Came to a little place called Downe.

'Darwin used to hang out here,' she said.

(Nearly asked Darwin who? Then remembered thankfully in time lead singer of that aristocratic pop group.)

Went in small pub called Queen's Head.

Sat on horsehair sofa in window and looked out at leafless trees and cold, quiet street feeling flattered by her attention. After all, I'm older than she is and not even a permanent worker in the family firm.

She came back from the bar with two Barley Wines and I thought Oo-er and took it slow. When she didn't speak I asked, 'Something I just said?' and she laughed and laid her hand over mine and squeezed it.

I felt honoured. As Dad once said, having shook the hand of our late King when he was Duke of York, I shall never wash again.

'Just a bit absent,' the princess beside me now said. Well, I could see that.

We had another drink and the sky outside grew darker until the panes by the sofa was just black squares. Wondered if Stanley would find the cod in the fridge, also frozen peas and whether he'd have enough savvy to heat the fat in the chip pan hot enough to make himself proper chips.

Excused myself and went to find a phone and called home. He thought oven chips were to do in the oven, for God's sake.

After a little Larch loosens up and we talked about the office and if I was happy there and about home and if I was happy there. Dodged that one, none of her damn business even if she is slumming, Lady Muck. She got a bit restless after that and asked me if I was hungry.

'I know it's early for dinner,' she said. 'But how about some Chinese food?'

I thought she meant takeaway and I said fine because I like to eat early partly because I'm always hungry and partly it gives you a nice long evening in front of telly and to do your nails.

So we ended up in Sevenoaks and by that time what with two Barley Wines inside me, reckoned we wouldn't meet that stallholder where we was going and I was right.

Went to a posh restaurant well away from market with all soft music and pretty, slant-eyed waitresses in black. She ordered for us both and a caraff of house plonk while we waited.

'Tell me about Stanley,' she says.

But something in me didn't feel inclined.

'Works for DemiPlan in Lewisham,' I said.

She signalled for another caraff. Going through the first like no tomorrow.

'Any good to you?' she asks lightly and for a moment I thought she meant the wine.

'Wouldn't have married him if not,' I answered, purposely misunderstanding her. 'We've always split fifty-fifty.'

'No, no,' she said laughing merrily and pouring herself more wine. 'I meant in bed.'

The cheeky cow. She signalled for another caraff, this time for me. My own personal one. Don't know why she didn't just order their whole cellar, would have saved her a bit of time.

Think she saw she'd gone too far when I didn't answer. Still, the starters came then, spare ribs in a red, gooey sauce. They smelt foreign.

'Use your fingers,' she says, seeing me looking.

'I was brought up to use a knife and fork,' I said.

'Well so was I,' she answers. 'And a spoon and fork for the pudding, but not for spare ribs.'

I always thought it was vulgar to say 'pudding'.

She started noshing into the spare ribs and getting ketchup on her pretty face.

'Been on a diet?' I asked sympathetically.

'No,' she said, looking up with her mouth full. 'Why?'

'Thought you seemed hungry.'

'I am,' she replied, swilling from her glass with fervour.

'No lunch, perhaps?'

'God, yes. Whacking great big one. Stew, then Spotted Dick and egg custard. Nanny knows my favourites. She's still at home, you see, looking after my grandfather. I went to see them today.'

I thought that was nice. But I was puzzled why her gran should be strange for being home.

'Don't you ever put on weight?' I asked her.

'No,' she said, filling up my wine glass. 'Well, go on. You were just about to tell me about Stanley.'

I was, Miss Impudence? I thought.

Sipped at my wine and waited for the pancake roll and beansprouts and looked at her. I thought, I got you taped; you're a (beautiful, elegant, upper-class) Nosey Parker. A clairvoyant, a *voyeuse*.

She got outside the pancake roll. Beansprouts flew right and left.

61

'My sex life is a mess,' she said, sighing, a bit martyr-ish and I thought Like your table manners, Madam.

'Gross feeder, aren't I?' she said smiling, and I was reminded of something Stanley once said about lettuces on his allotment. And then I thought of Auntie Beat who'd been a children's nurse when she was young.

'It was people like my Aunt Beatrice taught your sort to behave at table,' I said straight out.

'Didn't succeed in my case,' she said laughing and filled up the glasses again.

I wanted Black Forest Gato then but there wasn't any. We had some more wine and a brandy to follow. Wanted to say, 'Did you ought?' to her as she was driving, but didn't like to.

And then I said something I regretted later.

'Men...' she had begun.

'Yeah,' I said agreeing, girls together like, nothing more. 'Dunno why we put up with the sods, do you?'

She was crumbling bread at the time but she stopped right there and looked up, eyes alert. But she never said a word, and it was her silence made me go on.

'All that fuss...' I said. I was thinking of the little red cracker BIG BOY boxer shorts. 'I mean, the way they shout the odds about their things.'

Her eyes gleamed strangely. 'Go on,' she says.

'Well, that's it, really. No one special, they're all the same. Lot of shouting about nothing very much.'

'You're angry,' she says softly.

Angry? Well, if I was, it was ancient anger. Being told nice girls didn't only to find out nice girls got to later on. By which time the guilt was off the lily and no mistake.

'It was all contrairy messages when I was young,' I said, thinking. 'Still is. You dressed up and all they did was mess your ironed clothes. You'd save up for a nice bra and they'd break the strap or something. You'd get slim for 'em so they could make you fat with a baby. Nothing's fair.'

She smiled.

'Women always did get the damp patch. But you love your child.'

'That's different,' I told her. 'Though God knows nobody in their right minds . . . Not putting you off, am I? But the other's messy and it's silly. All those bums going up and down, up and down . . .' I remembered we were out and looked around suddenly. But nobody seemed to have heard.

She was laughing a bit oddly and beckoning for the bill. Soon after we were outside on the pavement under the cold stars, and I'd never offered to go dutch. Too late now. We began to walk towards the car.

'Great evening,' I said, to thank her.

'I enjoyed it too,' she said, and slipped an arm round my waist.

'I can manage, thanks,' I pointed out. Well, I hadn't had nearly so much to drink as she had. Pulled myself away, then saw I had offended her. Maybe she needed some support.

Didn't talk much on the way home. She just dropped me off outside the house and said good night and see you. Didn't ask her in.

Place in darkness and a smell of fish. He must have gone up to bed.

I tiptoes upstairs and creamed my face off in the bathroom. He was all warm and sleepy, but woke up when I got into bed and felt for the (stone) pig.

'That you?' he asked.

'No, it's the Princess Royal and you got the bed,' I told him. 'Move.'

'You smell of drink and minty toothpaste. Where you bin?'

'Out.'

'I know that. Where out?'

'Chinkychonk,' I said and reached for him and made him sleep spoons the way we do.

Will say this for Stan – short and podgy he may be

and with a belly on him but he isn't half nice to cuddle up to winter nights. Better than electric blanket any day. When he's not giving you loadsa bunny about where you been, that is.

You can keep that Nigel Havers.

Gimme chins.

Office Party. Cleared filing cabinets back and put desks by walls. Off at four, back six thirty with 'im in my oyster without jacket wore to wedding but jewellery instead. He fairly presentable in dark lounge. Bob and Mr Meredith from Accounts in white polos, looking as if lost submarines.

Garbo coming round with tray, saying, 'Crudities, anyone?'

Danced with Bob then saw Larch Mulliner arrive, tray glam with several men and glitter in her hair. I was partaking sparingly of dry white wine because of my new figure. She ignored me.

Had another d.w.w., then decided I wasn't having any silly old nonsense from her so waltzled up to her with Stanley and introduced them.

Quite forgot I'd told her my views on men and sex.

She gave him the once over and then they danced while I watched, worried in case he put a foot wrong, metaphysically speaking. She kept glancing round at me. And then heat started in my neck and rushed up into my face and she smiled and I felt all sorts of a fool and turned away. But not before she'd seen.

She smiled.

After that she was extremely nice to me. Said how we must meet up after Christmas.

Can't quite make her out.

Titchy little cheap square cards all round, though not for the two bitches, and that's Christmas in the office.

Garbo gave me a box of soap and talc.

Sauce.

One moment Christmas Eve, everything ready and nothing spoilt yet. Sideboard laden with apples and oranges I'd polished (should have done his head an' all) red wax candles in their glass holders, light on holly and ivy, pine scent of Christmas tree in central heating . . .

Wished moment would last for ever.

'Seems right carol singers should turn up now,' I said to him. 'And the first flakes of snow begin to fall.'

'Have a heart,' he said.

'Trouble with you is you got no romance.'

'Trouble with you is you believe in illusion.'

'It may all be illusion,' I said, quoting Aurora North-Brightley. 'But without it, who shall be brave?'

'Married you, didn't I?' he said.

Left it.

'Aunties Vi and Florrie in the morning,' I reminded him.

'You didn't ask Uncle Eamonn?'

'Not bloody likely. Anyway, no one's sure where he is right now. He got chucked out of that Salvation Army Hostel.'

'Oh. Well, be of good cheer,' he said. 'It's only four days after all.'

And with that my lovely moment went, never to return.

Dorelia round early Christmas Day, bless her, pretty in frilly dress, maternity, though she don't need it yet. Reminded me of when she was a little dot – that's how I used to dress her – jigging up and down, singing, 'We all Live in a Yellow Sumperine, Yellow Sumperine, Yellow . . .' and trying to snap her fingers.

Had stuffed turkey. She did sprouts and I got into making timetable for the cooking.

He off to collect aunts from Greenline as no trains.

Countess said she'd come by taxi, our Metro not big enough. Quart in pint pot.

Auntie Vi arrived, skinny arms full of parcels. Looked like praying mantis from *The Wildlife Show*. Flo flopped in after her. Funny how we run to lean and lard in our family. I mean, look at me and Amy.

Vi had a small sherry – well, she always starts slowly – and I and D. got the bird in and the pudding on. I'd done the table the night before and if I say it myself it did look nice. Got the idea from *Good Housekeeping*.

Went back into lounge and there they all were, Stan taking up the fireplace saying nothing, the aunties staring into space. Wayne in an armchair, drinking sherry and reading the *TV Times*.

'What's this, a morgue in here?' I cried. 'Everyone damn well jolly up!'

Well they shifted about a bit, but not very willingly. Wayne got up, dropping the *TV Times*, which Aunt Flo grabbed. Stanley got off the fire. Auntie Vi said, 'Let's be naughty!' leering hideously and holding out her glass.

'Stanley!' I said. 'Put on my King's College tape! Wayne, do the honours with the sherry. All be a bit more festive, for God's sake!'

Burst three balloons getting more sherry out from under the sideboard (didn't want to spoil my arrangement on the top). Found Aunt Florrie's shoes under there where she had kicked them.

'And turn the heating up,' I said to Stan. 'Hand round the nuts and crisps.' (Didn't want Vi drunk silly before Countess got here. She looks down on my relatives enough as it is.) 'Straighten your tie and get that big chair in from the hall.'

He started to say, 'What do you think I am, a bloody juggler?' when just then the Countess come, blocking out all the light and making everyone else, including Florrie, look very small.

Stanley went forward to kiss her.

66

'Hello Mum,' he said, all no enthusiasm and I wanted to kick his backside. She is his mother and it is Christmas after all.

She was all little smiles under her moustaches, delving deep into an old wicker shopping basket she'd brought and coming up with presents, though she knows we always leave that till everybody's here.

Wayne got her a sherry, but she waved it away.

'Never touch the stuff!' she says, lying old boot. 'Isn't there any fresh orange juice in this house?' And she looked pointed at my sideboard, where there was everything but.

Now I knew for a fact she'd had enough sherry last Christmas to sink the *Titanic* and still have enough left over for this season. May she be forgiven.

Slippers again for me.

Kiss her? When those long soft curly whiskers tickle so? Kissed air six inches from her cheek.

She unwrapped the headscarf I'd given her and held it up to the light to make sure that it was silk. (It was.)

'This must be my hundred and tenth,' she says, laughing lightly to show she wasn't really being spiteful. 'But thank you all the same. It'll go nicely with my collection.'

Fat old cow.

Had arranged to dish up at two so as to get The Queen in with the pudding. Flo flomped out to the kitchen to help but Vi and the Countess sat on in the lounge, swilling sherry and getting at each other in a polite sort of way for openers. Knew what they were doing. Didn't need to be in there watching.

King's College, Cambridge, Choir changed to Pet Shop Boys and then Def Leppard. D. must have gone in to break the old girls up.

Roderick and my dear Sister arrived with the little nameless dog. Fortunately Plum out. I said, 'You're early!' annoyed they were so late, and Amy hugged me long and hard and whispered, 'Merry Christmas!'

'Merry Christmas, Porky!' Roderick said, and kissed me

and added they'd been carol singing with the Sally Bash up Bromley Hospital.

Well, even the Countess smiled when Amy came in. The mood of the meeting changed. Aunt Flo found her shoes, Wayne poured more sherry and as dear Indira Candy might have said, it was a happy and relaxed family that sat down to Christmas dinner.

Well, sort of happy and relaxed.

Wayne uncorked the Asti for the elderly and the Countess said, 'Champagne? We *are* celebrating!' And Amy said softly, 'Yes, Christ's Birth,' which stopped the old bat's farting in church for a bit.

Stanley carved. Turkey nicely done. Didn't use Paxo this year.

Aunt Vi, well away by now, raised her glass and said, 'To the Cook!' which was nice, then Aunt Florrie raised hers and said, 'God bless us, everyone!' and then Vi was right back with '*Sod* Tiny Tim!' which offended the Countess very obviously.

Don't know why. Vi does it every year.

Stan laughed till the tears ran down.

Well, we had the pudding and The Queen, God bless her, and Aunt Vi sort of blubbed away quietly, being a monarchist and puggled. S. got a bit emotional too. Ah, but will they all when it's King Charles?

Had fruit, then nuts and crackers and sat on among the bits. Wayne went round with more wine, then D. and I cleared and got coffee. Suddenly the Countess said to D., 'Showing a bit, dear, aren't you?'

I would have hit her, but Dorelia just said, 'Surely you know the facts of life, Granny?' which shut her up and pleased me, knowing about *her*. She nonplussed her way through a portion of coconut, long whiskers blowing in a sort of emotional breeze. And then Auntie Florrie had to go and spoil it all.

'I had to get married,' she said dreamily to Dorelia. 'Same as you.'

68

The Countess pricked up her hairy ears. First she'd heard about Florrie, though she probably suspected about D.

There was a little pause.

'Seems to run in Cockney families,' the Countess said.

I could have thrown the table at her.

'*Middle Class*,' I said, remembering I was 'ostess. Well, Kitchener Close and all. Hardly proles.

Wrong thing to do.

'You don't want to be ashamed of your roots, my gel,' Aunt Vi said, wagging a finger while the Countess watched delightedly. 'Your farver weren't ashamed of it and neither was your mother. You and your Middle Class!'

'*Petit Bourjeois*,' Wayne put in, trying to be helpful.

The Countess loomed very big in her chair and preened her moustache. Because her grandfather had a draper's and outfitter's in the Strand last century she acts she's above us socially. But it's all a false facade.

(One thing: she don't know that I know what she's hiding. Keeping that secret like until I really need it.)

'Anyway, Wayne and Dorelia intended starting a family straight away,' I said, looking her in the eye.

'Oh no we didn't, Ma,' Wayne said.

Could of clocked him.

'We played Russian Roulette and lost, but since we're both very pleased now about the result and as we're the only two people it concerns, let's talk about something else.'

Amy said, 'Mary was pregnant when she married Joseph,' as if that finished the whole thing. Waited to see if the Countess would ask 'Mary and Joseph? More of your relations, I presume?' But she didn't.

All she said was 'Some single mothers keep their babies these days,' and I waited and Stanley looked at her sharpish, but she looked back at him straight, daring him to speak and he started fiddling with the tablecloth.

69

Worm.

We'd stacked up on the draining board when she came thundering out saying, 'Where's this new dishwasher we keep hearing about, then?'

Pointed to Stan.

'Still using my old one,' I told her.

'Do you mean *my son* is going to do the dishes?'

'No, *my husband*,' I said, catching Amy's eye and laughing.

This also happens every Christmas, for Pete's sake.

All the same, felt a bit sorry for Stan alone in the kitchen with his pile of plates so started with him. Then Dorelia came out and the aunts and Amy and we all mucked in except the Countess. Wouldn't have been room for her with us six anyway.

She lumbered off to the lounge to put first claim on the TV and D. got the giggles and dropped one of my Willow Pattern side plates. Told her she should put her feet up, being that way and she said, 'With Granny? Noway!'

Then Roderick and Wayne came in with Fella on his lead and he went mad seeing Amy. Then we all went in the lounge with the Countess.

Vi sat on the settee between her and Florrie, a sort of thin filling in a sandwich, which set D. off again. Wayne by some Christmas miracle got the control away from the old bat and switched channels to cover D.'s laughing and said, 'Oh, it's Wogan. I thought it was Bob Wankhouse,' which didn't do D. any good but just the reverse.

She went off to get her guitar from her bedroom and we had some carols after that, she plays so prettily. I was all right until we got to *Once in Royal*, then there's that line 'Where a mother laid her baby in a manger for His bed.'

It always does things to me. Went out into the hall and blubbed into the coats.

After a bit the lounge door opened and it was Stanley. Didn't say anything, just put his arms round me.

I said, 'Oh, I *hate* fucking Christmas!' and he said, 'Yes, I know, Mog. I know.'

Darren would have been twenty nine two days ago.

When we went in again Wayne was fooling about with mistletoe. Even held it above the Countess' head. Told him later he should have VC.

Then he went round with the port and D. put some of her father's Glen Miller stuff on and Vi and Florrie danced.

You never seen anything so funny. D. nearly wet herself. Even the old boot was smiling. Then Roderick and Wayne joined the aunties and the dog ran about barking. Then me and Stan got up – and that finished Dorelia. Thought she'd have the baby there and then. Poor Plum came nosing in and shot off out again, and Amy went to feed him and Fella tried to go too and got tangled up with the aunts.

We played Pit after that. The Countess dozed. I left the Bull and the Bear out but even so there was a lot of noise. Wayne went round filling up everybody's glasses and I kept getting corners in Wheat and Amy in Flax, and Roderick accused us both of insider dealing.

We yelled a good deal and the old girl woke up and grumbled but Wayne was right there with the port and she soon stopped. There was no more mention of fresh orange juice, I noticed.

Then I got supper. Made a lovely huge pot of tea and piles of ham and mustard sandwiches but Wayne went round with the brandy and nobody touched the cake.

Had sudden, sharp thought about Larch Mulliner – would she be doing this sort of thing now, at home with Nanny and Grandad?

Wayne did the brandy round again.

Whispered to him, 'Hey, steady on, there's tomorrow as well, you know,' and he whispered back, 'Don't worry, Ma. Got bootful of the stuff outside.'

'Wayne, you're the nicest son-in-law I've ever had,' I told him.

71

'Ma, I'm the only son-in-law you've ever had,' he said.

Well, the Countess thawed out at last and when Wayne asked her to dance, bowing over her hand like Sir Percy Blakeney, I nearly died, though I feared for the lounge floor.

Carried my poor cake out to the kitchen again and when I went back Wayne was doing another round with the brandy.

Dorelia played some heavy rock and I said, 'Haven't you any Chris de Burgh?' We argued and then played some early Beatles numbers, ones with tunes. The Countess ordained to say she quite liked these modern groups, which set Dorelia off again. She even kissed her grandmother. Just hope it don't affect the baby.

R. and A. and W. and D. left about twelve, leaving cars. Told both lots to give me three rings of the phone to let me know they were home.

Stood to watch them go then went back. Stanley was saying to the aunts we'd put them in the Blue Room, ho, ho, ho, and Flo beetled up tootsweet to get Dorelia's bed and leave the folding camp bed for Vi.

Countess got Put-U-Up in lounge. Grumbled at being woken up to go to sleep again.

Tidied things all round so as to be ready for the morning when fun will start again and she deliberately strewed her night and toilet things about, demanding a hot bath.

'I can't face it,' I told him when we were in our bed. 'Just can't face another day of having to be jolly.'

''Course you can, Mog,' he said. 'Easy. Besides,' he added, 'it's not just another day, it's *three*.'

Lay awake for some time wondering at this 'Mog' business. Moggy was the slimline girl he courted. What's he after?

Listened to the snoring belting up the stairs from down below. Then clear and shrill the phone bell sounded, cutting through. The snoring stopped, surprised, faltered a bit and then began again, until it was interrupted by another three shrill rings. This time it stopped for good.

Lay awake a little longer, picturing the Countess, great bulk squeezed into unfamiliar hard bed, trying to get to sleep and possibly wondering if the blasted phone was going to ring yet again, a sort of Irishman's boot.

Chuffed.

Boxing Day worse – *Uncle Eamonn.*

Roderick said, 'Christ!' looking out of the window about half eleven and when I looked too, didn't have the heart to reprove him.

The old boy was weaving about in Kitchener Close, sometimes on the pavement, more often in the road, hanging over gates and looking up at houses as if the right one, when he found it, would introduce itself.

R. went to get him in. He said, 'Merry Crish – Crish – I've forgotten.' He'd had so much to drink by the time he got to us he piddles all round the toilet making lakes on my nice carpet. Wayne said, 'At least he got to the bathroom.' But I couldn't see the sense of that remark.

Didn't have any presents for him but that didn't matter as he certainly didn't have any for us.

He was sick on the landing. Plum ran up and sniffed at it and Aunt Vi screamed, and Dorelia laughed, though later found she had thrown up too. Amy said must be charitable, poor old Uncle lives all on his own. Roderick said not surprised.

Only the Countess had a wonderful time looking down her sprouting nose at my family. When he didn't even recognize Sister Vi she laughed aloud.

'Dorelia,' I said about tea time. 'Got any vitamin pills, sweetheart?'

'Yes,' she says, giving me a look. 'Why?'

'Bloody Christmas,' I said.

'But everything's just as usual,' she says, astonished.

'That's why I want 'em,' says I.

'Poor Mummy. Perhaps you're going through the Change.'

73

'Perhaps.'

She thought hard, as if searching for something to cheer me up.

'And here's me with my little girl,' she says at last.

Girl?

'Had a scan,' she said. 'Been meaning to tell you. I asked and they told me. Pleased?'

Pleased? I'd thought I wouldn't give a stuff what it was as long as she was all right and happy but suddenly there it was, I was right over the moon.

'We all move up,' I said, struggling not to show how pleased I was. 'Me into my old mother's place, you into mine, and now . . .' I hugged her. 'Then of course, someone has to fall off the edge to make room,' I said, and she laughed.

'What you going to call her?' I was hoping for Yolanda or Evadine or Anastasia.

'Jane.'

'Jane? Jane Dorelia, you mean?'

She shuddered. 'Just Jane.'

Well, I'd had a faint, faint hope of Jane Noreen, but something told me to put that one away fairly fast.

'Wayne pleased it's a girl?' I said.

'Oh yes,' said my daughter. 'He's a New Man, remember?'

I read somewhere that even the weariest river winds to the sea at last. That's how it was. And now, here I am with a Tupperware box of turkey mince, three unpulled crackers, a droppin' fir tree and Uncle Eamonn asleep on the army bed upstairs. (Won't let him use Dorelia's.)

Oh, and a new pair slippers and a new, new, *new* giant, (though not Economy) size bottle White Satin with a label on a ribbon round its neck saying 'Mog'.

H'mmm.

Eamonn says his pension's run out. But it's him that done

a runner. At least in the hostel he had to shave. Now he looks like something David Bellamy found.

Stan ratty and can't blame him.

Amy will have to have Eamonn. She doesn't have a job.

Soon will have, though.

Eamonn moved to A. and R.'s. We all went to put his name down for place in Council Old Folks' Home, but he doesn't qualify for one reason and another. Still, Amy doesn't have a job.

Decorations tatty, annoying me so took them down. Place looks bare. He said 'Twelfth Night ain't for days yet!'

Mulliner's closed until 2nd Jan. .

Very dull and flat.

''Reen,' he said to me in bed last night. ''Reen, I'm bursting with it, you know that?'

'Bursting with what?' I murmured – reading *Passion's Destiny* by dear Aurora and irritated at being disturbed.

'You know.'

'No I don't.'

'Yes you do.'

Sighed and closed Aurora, though I kept hold of her, with a finger in my place.

'Well, be quick and get it over with,' I said.

'You turn me right off, you know that?' he said. 'Whassa matter, don't you love me no more?'

'Daft ha' porth,' I said.

Sighed again and put the light out, but he was huffy.

'Come on,' I told him, reaching for him all resigned.

He wouldn't.

Why can't he be like Sir Sacheverel de Mandeville who besides vigorously deflowering the female population of his county, put his entire London house-hold in pod, insisted on his conjugal rights with Lady Mandeville ('An heir, Evangeline, I must have an heir!') and still had strength to try and knock off the governess, the heroine?

Told Stan about Sir Sacheverel.

'That's rape,' he said shortly and turned over.

So it is.

Sometimes I feel all alone, living in a backwater or some-thing, one of the lonely places of the world. Life, such as it is, passing me by.

Haven't done anything to be proud of. Oh, there's Dorelia, she's my best, she's bright and pretty and her legs are straight, but what's it all about? Another little person coming, and what for?

We're born and then we live and then we die.

Why?

And I'm afraid of things, things that didn't use to bother me, like falling off the edge of the world at times. Can't say these things to him. Can't say them to anybody.

Sometimes wake up with a vague surprise I'm me instead of someone else. Looking at life through grey-coloured spectacles, those mornings.

No, I can't tell him. He'd just say, 'We'll have a nice cuppa tea,' or 'Blimey, you want cheering up, let's go down the pub and see Dora.'

After thirty years I know him from toupée to nuts.

Is there life after death? If I knew there was and I should see little Darren again, maybe things wouldn't seem so bad.

Went down the Group Practice Surgery and old Dr McCleod told me to pull myself together. Wanted to smack him in the gob.

Stared.

'You ought to get yourself a job instead of polishing

and gossiping all day,' he said severely.

Wherever has he been living the last twenty years?

I said, 'I got a job and somebody's got to polish.'

He said, 'It's all in your head, you know.'

Burst into tears.

He got worried then and rang the bell for the nurse, but I run out before she could come in. Dunno what the people outside thought – I been told I got terminal cancer or summing. Stood outside and leaned against the wall round that little garden thing they got there and cried and cried.

Presently the nurse come out and touched me on the arm and asked if she could help.

'Oh, it's *him*,' I said, jerking my head at the Surgery. 'Silly old ponce saying it's all in my head. 'Course it is, I know that and I want something for it on the National Elf.'

'You might be better off seeing Dr Bennett,' she said. 'A lady doctor, about forty. I'll make you an appointment.'

Dried my eyes. Later saw this Dr Bennett who said to take Vitamin E so I got these custardy-tasting things from Boots, but they didn't do no good. Everything feels much the same. Dorelia says they're not the natural form of the vitamin and anyway, Boots experiments on animals and anything come from suffering bound to do no good.

Threw bottle away.

He asked me how I was. I said 'Don't raise your hopes.'

He said 'I'd better go and cut it off, then, eh?' And I told him 'No need to be so drastic. Tie a knot in it, why don't you, just as good and won't hurt half so much.' Well, you gotta laugh.

He didn't think it was all that funny, though.

New Year

Found Aunt Flo's Christmas shoes down the settee.

77

Posted them on to her, then realized she might think belated present coming, so phoned.

She said, 'Where's Eamonn?'

I said, 'Round Amy's.'

She said, 'Can she cope?'

And I said, 'Case of have to, innit?'

After all, Amy hasn't got a job.

He's got three new waggons, one a biggie with 'Palethorpe's Sausages' down the side, one white one that says, 'Glass-Lined United Dairies Milk Tank', and a little, open, grey one with 'Roberts Davy. Ask for Prices' on it.

Ask for Prices? I just bet he did, the train shop girl.

And what I'd like to know is, whom is kidding who?

'They had a sale, 'Reen,' he said. 'Really.'

Oh?

Roderick and my dear Sister asked us over New Year's Eve. Thought at first we wouldn't go as it means walking, he not wanting to get picked up and spend a night in the cells. Told him he could always drink juice, but he looked so miserable I said we'd walk.

When Roderick opens a new whisky bottle he throws the cork away all casual over his shoulder and don't bother to find it. And never pours out less than a tumblerful at a time.

So me and mine walked up through Anerley along the A213 under railway arch which reads *Spurs Wank True* and on into darkest Penge, which R. pronounces *Parnje*, a la Francay.

No one about. Police down side streets waiting.

'Be a different picture later on,' he said, nodding wisely.

Roderick opened the door with wreath of ivy round his head and Fella yapping, quite at home (also with ivy wreath) and totally other than poor little cruelly treated thing. It stopped you getting pissed according to ancient legend he said.

Thought privately he and the little dog seemed to have

78

been testing this theory for some time. Dog's breath smelt of beer.

Stan said, 'Blimey, need summing stronger than ivy, New Year,' and I was inclined to agree.

'Only way to separate the cream from the crap,' said Roderick, gracefully waving a hand. 'The empirical approach.'

Ah.

My dear Sister, very slim in clean jeans and a Garfield sweatshirt, was on diet Coke. R. handed me a glass of the Glenlivet just like a cheque from the Pools. I put some of Amy's diet Coke in to water it down.

Their next doors came in, two young doctors, black – well, olive brown. Very middle class. Wanted to talk to the girl about me and Vitamin E but didn't because it's rude to do that at parties.

About half eleven R., with ivy leaves any old how, thereby disproving ancient legend, said, 'What about the horse trough? Up enda Glenda, anyone?' And I trans-related for him in case the little doctors thought it was something not quite nice.

I said, 'At the end of Glenda Jackson Avenue where the road forks, there's an old horse trough, been there hundred and fifty years. The Council put flowers in it in summer, red white and blue, ever so tasteful and patriotic. In the New Year all us local people dance round it and sing *Olde Lang Syne*. It's an ancient English custom,' I told them, for I was on my third or fourth whisky and after that first one I didn't dare add Coke because Roderick had seen what I was doing and had thrown some awful kind of Scottish fit. 'It dates back to the time of Henry II,' I said, which wasn't quite true. We only thought of it last year.

'Lots of mediaeval things round here,' I went on, looking at Stanley and keeping a straight face.

Roderick bellowed '*Conga!*' then and we all joined up and went round the house and garden. Told the doctors it was another ancient custom.

There was already a crowd at the horse trough when our Conga arrived, laughing and kicking, and Roderick organized the ring. Easy with his height. And when Big Ben struck (someone had brought a tranny) we had *Olde Lang Syne* and the tears come in my eyes.

Well, it was lovely till the trouble started. But somebody was high and punched somebody and then somebody threw an empty lager can and before you knew it there were bottles whizzing and the traffic which had come up and couldn't get through started hooting and then a single, full bottle smashed a windscreen. Then there was another one, and with the second smash, the Cavalry arrived.

Two of the sodium lights at the junction went out and after that, though it wasn't dark, it wasn't easy to see. I lost Stanley and then saw him again suddenly. He was standing between two youths and they seemed to be giving him hassle.

I started to run forward, but somebody grabbed my arm – Roderick.

'Not a good idea,' he said. 'I'll go.'

Well, everything might have been all right then, but a copper got hold of Stan under the impression he was the one causing aggro. The two youths tried to melt away, but could hardly move for the crowd.

That copper went on holding our Stanley.

I wriggled free of Roderick suddenly and worked my way through the crush round to the back of the action and first I kicked hard at the back of those yobboes' legs (used to do that to girls in front of me in School Assembly, no wonder I was top of list of Expulsions Pending) and then I kicked the policeman's.

All buckled up like tower blocks under demolition. The cop fell on the top, pinning the tangle to the ground. And Stanley, thinking fast for once, whirled round, got my hand and pushed me into the crowd. R. caught us up (he'd been after me) and we thumped our way through to the edge where it was thin and a young policewoman was standing by a white patrol car looking on.

'Nasty element in there tonight,' Roderick told her sadly. 'We're leaving, I'm afraid. Goodnight, Officer. Happy New Year.'

He sounded really pained. But he was careful to keep in front of me so she didn't see my face.

She was so bothered she didn't answer. Poor thing, I thought, they didn't ought to have girls deal with rowdies. Then Roderick taking each of us by an elbow either side of him, hurried us down Glenda Jackson fast as we could go.

'Bitta luck somebody whanging that copper,' my Stanley observes, between puffs.

'Me, you trog,' I said, and Roderick said, 'Serious offence, assaulting a constable.'

'We got away,' I pointed out coldly.

I've noticed before men can't stand for women to have a successful part in the action.

'Yeah, but they're bound to come looking for you,' R. said. 'Along with all the other hooligans.'

'I'll tell them it was me kicked their legs from under them,' Stan said.

We got to the house then and Amy flung open the door. No sign of the nice little doctors.

I said to him, 'Twat. You were in front of them. It was my speciality did it, kicking them from behind.'

Roderick said to me, 'Why don't you shut up? You should be glad the bloke offers to speak up for you.'

'Don't you go at her!' Amy told Roderick and then I turned on her.

'And you can leave *him* alone. If we hadn't had him we'd be up there still.'

'If we hadn't had him we wouldn't have *been* there,' Stanley said.

'Who ponced up and offered those yobs bovver?' Roderick demanded.

81

Sometimes sodding Christmas just goes on and on and on.

Larch called me at work yesterday. Gave her a chance to hear my telephone voice. She giggled and said, 'Drongo, it's me. What about a drinkie-poo tonight?'

Well, I was pleased. Stanley could get his bloody own.

'Pick you up at eight, then. Your house.'

And then it was I had a little chill, a horrid sort of premonition thing.

'No,' I told her. 'Corner of Elmers End Road.' And I sat thinking and trying to find out what was wrong. I seemed to be in two or five minds at once.

Strange, when you can't say to yourself what it is you're thinking.

However, the phone went again and again after that, and I had to work all morning, which weren't right. I was simply *unindated* with phone calls.

Got so fed up I walked out early and took an hour and a half buying a new frock; dull red peplum in creep de sheen with padded shoulders and polyester mock-silk lining. Nobody said a dickybird when I got back with my bags. Wouldn't dare.

Stanley said he'd get his own and I whizzed off with Larch in the Gilbern. She didn't want anywhere local this time, which was just as well as the icky feeling was still with me. Told myself it was because my patch was all working class and not good enough, but that wasn't really it, not by a long chalk.

'Expect you're fancying somewhere a bit more stylish,' I said to her, testing the water. 'Where the beautiful people go?'

She nodded and half smiled.

And still the weirdo feeling stuck with me.

She drove across the river and through Chelsea, and then parked in a side street on a meter. I got out and looked round for the beautiful people, but she grabbed my hand and led me up to a place hidden in a wall, dead scruffy, with garage sort of doors.

When she knocked a fattish young man with boobs – 'mantits' my Stanley calls them – opened, looked us up and down, knew her and let us in, all without smiling. Foreign feeling came on stronger than ever.

We went down a staircase and she signed a book. There was a bar there in a darkened room with Joan Armatrading coming from the juke box. Place looked like a cave.

Asked me what I'd like to drink but didn't listen and came back with Barley Wine. There was another fattish chap behind the bar, but when I looked, I see it was the same one let us in.

'Thanks, Brenda,' said our Larch, and I thought Funny.

But even then I didn't savvy. A real dumb cluck, me.

For no special reason I was thinking about the Palethorpe's Sausages van on his model layout when suddenly a cold wind seemed to come at me from nowhere, wrap itself round me and chill me to the bone. I couldn't explain it to myself, I just knew it was connected some way with the fluffy bint in the train shop, and I sat there clutching my bit of frozen knowledge to me and wishing I was home.

Oh my God, I thought. There's vitally important things going on out there and I'm stuck down this poxy hole. Larch Mulliner said something to me and I nodded. The record on the juke box changed to a very old Joan Baez – I think. I pushed away the drink my friend had brought me.

Suddenly I stood up.

'I'm sorry, I got to go,' I told her. She looked up, surprise in her face.

'But my dear girl, we just arrived!'

'I know that,' I said. 'I'm sorry like I said, but to be honest with you . . .'

'Yes?'

I chickened out. 'I'm not feeling very well.'

She didn't believe me, I could see . . .

'Will the man on the door let me out?' I asked her, and she laughed.

'Why try to be funny? If you don't like the company, you're free to go.'

'Yes, but will he . . . ?' I had some idea the door at the the top of the stairs was kept locked.

'Oh, don't be so fucking naive!' she burst out. 'Be your age. This is The Gates.'

I stared at her and I went on staring. Must have looked a real gormless twit. Then I looked at the couples on the floor in the middle, dancing and necking and hanging on each other and by God there were no men there at all. Even the butchier types in heavy duty leather gear had swellings on their chests, Miss Sweetbushes to a woman, all of them.

She was watching me, pretending to be slightly amused still, but wary.

'Don't make a scene,' she said. 'Sit down. If it isn't too much trouble.' (Coming the old acid.)

I sat.

'That's better,' she says softly, putting a hand over one of mine. 'Playing hard to get is one thing, Noreen dear, but this act of yours is ridiculous.'

I felt stupidified. I was looking at the dancing and finding it silly; reminded me of youth club hops in the 'Fifties when there were never enough boys to go round. 'Course I always had one but those that didn't had to dance with each other. I'da died of shame, first.

'Surely you know why we came here,' Her Highness was saying. 'I've fancied you for ages, you must have seen. I simply have a *thing* about older women. Looking for a mother-figure I suppose.'

She was squeezing my hand, too tightly, the whole horrid/crazy biz beginning to dawn on me in slow

84

motion. Then I suddenly saw clear. I pulled my hand away.

'I thought you liked me too,' she said sadly, but the sadness was put on. She was watching me like a hawk.

'I do – did,' I said, and knew I hadn't really, only who she was and the sharp clothes she wore and the notice she'd taken of me.

Still, we knew what that was all about now, didn't we?

'There's been a mistake made,' I said.

'Oh? After all you told me about being unhappy with your husband, and not liking men?'

'I never,' I said, and as I said it I remembered, and could see how she'd thought . . . what she thought.

'You thought wrong,' I told her. 'I didn't mean it the way you thought I did.' I got up again to go.

'I'm devastated. But surely we can be civilized. Let's have a drink.'

'I got one.'

'Then have the manners to wait until I can join you,' she says, going over to Brenda and the bar.

Lady Muck.

I'd sat down again by the time she come back. Perhaps I did owe her 'explanation. She had a bottle with her this time, obviously intent on putting it away. I didn't touch my glass. For one thing I wanted a clear head. For another I think it would have made me sick.

'So you've decided you're not one of us,' she says, swilling.

'Never was.'

'Shouldn't knock till you've tried it. Believe me, it's better.'

'How better?'

'Gentler,' she says, closing her eyes. 'Sweeter. Much more emotional.'

'Beats me what you actually do.'

She opens her eyes very wide. 'Noreen, you ever *found* your fanny?'

85

'No need to talk dirty,' I told her, and stood up again. 'I'm off. I'm sorry it's turned out like this. It was a misunderstanding.'

'Go on, then,' she says, waving her glass. 'Go home to that fat little man. Wears a silly little hairpiece, doesn't he, and spits when he laughs? Go home to your sweet old-fashioned marriage, your cosy domesticity. Go home and get all excited about the new dishwasher coming – I know, because he retailed me with that and other enthralling details when we were dancing. What a lover he must make for you, so . . .'

'Don't you talk like that about him!' I said to her.

She laughed. And all the time she was drinking and watching me with the eyes of her narrowing in her face, not that they'd be doing it anywhere else.

'I'll go, then,' I said.

'Do,' she said, filling up her glass. The Joan Baez changed to Sarah Brightman. I walked across to the stairs.

She was still sitting there. As I watched she smiled and waved to someone in a dark far corner and then got up to join them, Noreen forgotten. I went up the stairs.

Grisly Boobs let me out at the top and I went and stood outside and shivered a bit. Then I walked back into the King's Road and got a taxi to Victoria.

He was sitting up in bed when I got in with a cup of tea and his trains annual.

'Nice evening?' he asked and when I didn't answer – 'You're all upset about something, aren't you?'

'Clever of you to notice,' I muttered (sarcasm) and got into bed and reached for the stone piggy we got from Cromer. He didn't look like a man who is having an affair, more like someone who's had his feet kicked off a warm place where he's had them.

'Wassup, Mog?' he asked and that did it. Now I knew.

86

He kept calling me Mog because he'd got something to hide. He was guilty as hell. I hit him.

It was either that or burst into tears so I hit him.

'What's that for?' he asked and I wanted to tell him, but instead I started to cry.

'Oh now, now,' he said. 'Now, now, now!' And of course that irritated me so I stopped. He gave me his cup of tea.

'Well, eyes down now for a good night's kip,' he said when I drunk it, but being told that kept me more wide awake than ever.

It was a long time before I got to sleep. Kept seeing Larch Mulliner and her considering, narrowed eyes.

Slept badly, and had to get out for a pee about four.

Work very strange this morning. No one wanted to chat or even give the time of day. Went out to lunch and came back only five minutes late and Garbo pointed to the clock and hemmed.

Sacked! Suzie from Personnel come up and said I needn't come in after Friday as Mulliner's new policy is to phase out temps and take on permanent.

Codswallop. Or *bloody* new silly policy – since I went to The Gates, if you ask me.

Thank God we're living in a paid-for house.

He nice about it, but could see it hit him. Pointed out we're very much better off than most. True. I said, though, 'You'll have to keep on doing dishes.'

He said, 'If that's the worst, who cares?'

I said still hoping for a holiday abroad.

He sighed.

Nice to be home all day again. He's nifty with the Hoover – I seen to that – but nobody does it like I do.

You can see kittens wriggling in our Plum, Nature I suppose. I give him extra cream and vitamins from the health shop same as D. and made him a lovely little bed all lined with dustbin bags and put in two of Stanley's Damarts for the top.

He said, 'I wanted those.'

'Forget them,' I told him. 'They aren't maco.'

He hopped a bit on one foot. Then he said 'Would you – know be different if I didn't wear them?'

'Them and your thermal socks,' I said, though I never thought he'd take the words to heart. I mean, he's been using underwear to sleep in all the years we've been doing it together.

'My father never wore socks in bed,' I said.

'Well, I'm not your father!' he said. 'Thank the Lord.'

'What you mean, Thank the Lord?' I asked, agreed, though I already knew.

'Yes,' he said, nodding with heavy meaning.

'What you mean, Yes?'

Well, he backed off then. Didn't want a full scale row.

'You know. Might have been better if he had worn clothes,' he mumbled, subsiding once more into the dogs-body I know and can handle.

'That'll do,' I said. 'He was a good father and all that.'

Well, so he was. It's just he had this other family over Orpington, or so someone took pains to tell my mother when he died. I don't know. Probably just a mischief maker. We never been to see.

Plum just sniffed at the beautiful made-up bed. Must be the smell of Stanley's vests.

Turned out the bedroom today. Found a mass of torn up paper under the bed. *Daily Mails*, *Here's Healths*, *Peg's Owns*, *Juicy Bits* . . .

Stood and stared at it in amazement. A lot of it punctu-ated with little holes. It was like those sheets you feed in those old violas.

Swept it all up and put in black plastic bag and hoovered up all the little pieces.

20th January

It's all come back, worse mess than before. Just bent down to get my slippers and there it was, just as if never cleared away. Stood and stared at it in amazement.

Got into bed still fazed and sat writing and waiting for him to come out of the bathroom.

Woken by little grunts . . .

'She's having them,' Stanley said.

'Sh!' he went on and turned on his light and hung out like a prawn in a cocktail, counting.

'Looks like four,' he said, coming up. 'I think she's finished. Eating up the mess now.'

'She what?'

'You know the facts of life, surely,' he said, sounding like Dorelia.

I lay back against the pillow. 'Anything on my grey carpet?'

He went down again. 'No. She's licked it all up.'

'He's a little cannibal,' I said.

'She, 'Reen, *she*,' he said and went off to get Plum top off the Gold Top milk.

'You in a good mood, 'Reen?' he asked when he come back.

'Not in a bad one.'

'Well, then?'

'Well, what?'

'What about a bit?'

'You still got your socks on,' I pointed out. 'And anyway, I got 'eadache.'

And that's how it was the night Plum's kittens were born – *stalemate*. Oh, very funny. But I didn't laugh much as I went to sleep.

Towards dawn I come up through the layers of it and saw the little bitch told Mum the family in Orpington was there.

'They look elsewhere if they don't get it at home,' she was saying and I woke up thinking of model trains.

After a bit I moved towards him under the bed clothes. And found he'd put the thermal socks back on again.

Driven mad brooding on this no-win situation. Sent him out to get tobacco in clean trousers while I checked his others. Found a train shop receipt. Put it back.

Followed him up the shops. He went in paper shop and then came out and headed home. Didn't go in train shop in clean trousers. I nipped up alley and in back.

Always home one o'clock. Can't do a thing with him in the house.

Going through end pages local paper looking for jobs when found Personal Column.

Madame Bovary. Now there's a false name for you. (The real one was old Greek tart, that much I do remember from school.) *Clairvoyance, Tarot Cards, Palmistry*.

And she lived local. Addiscombe.

Thought why not? I'd give a good deal to see into the future. Also the present's a bit of a mystery to me.

Rang her up there and then, being alone in house, and made an appointment for ten days' time.

Honest to God, everything's flawed in this world. One of Plum's kittens, little female tabby, is blind. The other three, all boys, opened their eyes days ago. She just totters round blundering into things on her little legs.

And a local tom, maybe even kittens' father, keeps trying to come into house. Sprays on the cat door. Smell.

Roderick Attenborough McKay says after kittens, wants to slaughter toms before they grow big enough to threaten him.

Also Plum may come into season again quickly, but I don't think that can be true. You can't fall for another

90

baby while you're still breast-feeding the first one.
Everyone knows that.

Wanted to nail cat door up. Stan said plastic, so got sticky tape and put that across. Now let him try to come in.

Appointment with Madame B. for half six. Got his tea, then said I was off with a friend.
'What friend?' he asked, frowning.
Could be a man for all he knows.
Passed them next door who moved in. Couple of Larch Mulliners, if you ask me. Still, they said Good evening and hung about as if wishing to be civil. I walked on. Had enough with her and P.G. Wodehouse.

Madame Bovary in basement flat, stank of cats far worse than our back door. Thought of Plum back home and hoped he was seeing to her, letting her out when she has to go and kill things for her babies.
Can't be much money in telling fortunes else she'd have seen where one was and gone for it, ho ho.
Bloke who let me in was her husband. He went off to the kitchen where I could hear him getting meal. Then in she came.
Don't know what I expected – dark-eyed gypsy with skirts and gold earrings, I suppose. She mousey little thing in tatty woollen suit, permed hair. Still, said, 'Do come in, Mrs Spink,' every bit as pleasant and nice as that receptionist up the dentist.
Waved me to a chair behind a table and said 'I don't charge a fee.' And I gave a sigh of relief for though I'd brought a fiver with me, he didn't know and I felt a bit sly. Then remembered the train shop bit.
'But I do accept donations,' she went on. 'If you feel that what I tell you is significant, that is.'
Thought to myself we'd see what was significant. And

91

she must have seen my look, because she smiled.

Well, she examined the palms of my hands for starters and told me I had a long, vigorous life ahead and that I felt things keenly. Well, I could have told her that. Also I was married – brilliant, I was wearing my wedding ring.

Then she saw two children in my hand and I blurted out, 'One's dead,' before I could stop myself and she said just about to tell me that. Fiver appeared to be safer than ever.

She gimme look then and said we'd try the Cards and fetched them out where she'd got them hid, all wrapped up in a cloth and spread them on the table. They were big, crudely-coloured things with ugly pictures. Could have painted her better ones myself.

Asked me to shuffle and cut the pack three times, thinking as I did so about a particular problem. The particular problem wasn't hard. What bothered me was whether to add the words 'with the train shop girl'. Then thought the Cards would maybe know about that anyway.

She took the pack away from me and began to lay them down face up, in a sort of pattern on the table.

'This is you,' she says of the first one. 'In relation to the question you have asked.'

Well, it was someone in robes, going on a journey, holding a lantern up to find their way.

'Lonely,' says she. 'The Hermit. You are feeling for your way ahead. Something you thought was fixed in your life has changed. And your attitude towards it isn't right.

'And I cross it with . . . The Chariot.' Across the first card she laid a picture of someone driving a cart. 'This represents the obstacle in the question you have asked.'

Two horses were pulling that cart, trying to go different ways. Driver was looking bothered. Well, he would do.

'Someone's in two minds,' she says. 'There's a decision to be taken here.'

'Card Number Three,' she said, putting it to the top of the little cross, 'shows your conscious aim in this matter. *The Sun*. Light on your problem. And Card Number Four' – laying it underneath the cross – '*The Lovers*. Your subconscious aim.'

Well there was a lot more after that but to be honest she lost me though she put in a great deal of work with her 'field of relationships with others', her 'spiritual force behind the problem' and so on. Began to see how she might earn that fiver after all.

But then she turned the tenth and last card up which she said showed the outcome of it all and blow me, it was the Death Card.

A skeleton with a scythe was moving across a field chopping hands and feet off people. He'd done his own left foot an' all.

'Not what you think,' she says, looking sharpish at me. 'This card signifies change. Transformation, not death as it is traditionally accepted, the end of everything, but commutation into something finer. As, for example, caterpillars. Do we say they die when they pupate?'

'They do if a bird gets them,' I said.

'No, no! Not what I meant. Let us take wood or coal. What's left when we burn them is ash, but the essential atoms are still there. The point to observe here is that nothing stays the same for ever.'

Then she abandons the philosophy and it's back to the nitty gritty.

'This card means somebody has got to change their attitude.'

She gimme little lecture and I gave her that little fiver, kicking myself for being so bloody wet. Think she saw that though and offered me ten minutes with the crystal ball for extras. But I'd had enough by that time – nothing she'd told me was significant and I was bitterly disappointed – and I wanted out.

'Just one more thing,' she said to me as I was going. 'I've been seeing a large house with you ever since you arrived. Are you thinking of moving, by any chance?'

What, leave *Semper Idem*?

'Noway,' I said, buttoning my coat. 'He's got the garden just they way I like it and anyway I'm near my married daughter.'

Waited a minute or two to see if she'd see my little granddaughter in the large house but she only shook her head.

'Strange. It's very clear. And it's definitely with you. A very big house, one might almost call it a mansion, with an impressive hall. I can even see the flowers on the table, they're chrysanthemums in a bright brass jug. Armchairs – big leather ones. And a red Turkey carpet.'

I went to the door.

'Don't mean a thing,' I said. 'Sorry.' And wondered what I was doing, apologizing to her. What a waste of time. Still, the thing to do was get home now without being robbed further or even raped and murdered.

'Mind if I call a cab?' I asked her and she let me use her phone, watching me still and no doubt seeing this large house.

Anyone could get fivers doing what she done and doubtless it's not tiring like whoring.

'Where you bin?' he asked when I got in and I said, 'Out' before I noticed he was all upset.

' 'Smatter?' I said absently, picking up the electric bill which had come second post.

More satisfied customers! a note said with the bill.

Oh yeah? Not with the way they're digging up the road outside and getting dust in my front room, for which privilege we have to bloody pay.

'She . . .' he started and I looked up.

'Baby all right?' I asked swiftly.

94

'Far as I know,' he said. 'No, it's Plum. I was sitting here watching *Match of the Day* when that old tom cat must've broke in. I heard a noise and went out and your tape was all bust.'

'And where was Plum?'

'Out. I'd let her out some time before.'

'And did she come back in again?'

'Yes, later. I followed her upstairs for a Jimmy and looked in the bedroom and there it was.'

'What?'

'One of the kittens. Dead. It was lying on its side with its head all crooked. Died defending itself, I think.'

I left him there and belted upstairs. I could hear Plum crying softly before I even looked under the bed. (I'd moved them all out once, but Plum moved them back again.) She was licking one of the kittens which was dead like he said. There was a frozen snarl on its little face. If I'd had a brick in my hand I'd have smashed that old tom to a pulp.

I got the small body away from her. They can't count and the sooner she got on looking after the other three . . .

There were only two. Live ones, that is.

'Stanley!' I shouted down the stairs. 'Where's the other one?'

He come thundering up. 'Other what, 'Reen?'

'Other kitten, dummy. There were four. One's dead, that should leave three, right?

'I dunno,' he said, getting down on his hunkers and peering in at Plum. 'Search me.'

Nearly kicked him. He was easy target.

Then we look all over the house, every nook and cranny, but only two live kittens. Checked their back-sides. Males, like the one that died.

'It's the girl that's missing,' I said. 'The little blind one.'

'Oh shit,' my Stanley said.

Kitchener Close very dark and empty except for street lights making orange flower-splashes on damp pavement. A fine drizzle, sort of fog droplets falling. Didn't help.

He got his flashlight and we went about all hunched, looking in every corner of the garden. Called, 'Little girl! Little blind girl!' After the first five minutes didn't care what neighbours thought.

The Larch Mulliners next door came out. Asked if we'd lost something. He told them about the marauding tom. Nice and sympathetic. Got torch and came along too, up the allotments.

We quartered the ground and beat it the way you see them do a murder hunt on telly (well, what was this?) but it wasn't no use. He said he'd swing for that tom if he caught him. Voice of us all.

About midnight we give up and I asked them both in for a drink. Only civil, being so nice. But they looked at each other and said they got to get to bed. I went red hot, thinking what that meant. Which one of them was it said, 'Give us a bit'?

'Nice ladies,' he said going in our gate.

'Lezzies,' I told him and he said, 'Strike a light. How you know?' and I told him about Larch Mulliner. Hadn't before because felt such a fool.

'Bloody hell,' he said.

Wanted to do it but we run out of johnnies.

Lowered pride and went down Job Centre. Nothing. Windy. Cold. Fed up.

Back again. Saw man. Nothing. Fed up.

Back again. Nothing. Fed up.

Toyed with ad. in Personal Column: FAT LADIES WANTED FOR ROLYPOLY KISSAGRAMS. PHONE ESSENTIAL.

Well, I had the phone.

Job Centre called. How about Nursing Auxiliary over Belvedere Grange?

I said reluctantly no nursing experience, never been a nurse. He said not to worry, training given.

Interview tomorrow, three o'clock. Matron Peebles.

Snow.

Still snowing. Got bus. In hurry. Slipped. Laddered tights. *Fuck.*

Grange up hill in posh area Sydenham, well, was once, now all Victorian houses overgrown and gone to seed. Shabby flats with racks of doorbells, dead gloomy monkey puzzle trees and peeling paint.

Stopped under huge holly leaning out half over pavement and powdered nose.

Big, mature trees all round Grange, including dead elms. Also lots of dark laurel bushes and a sort of turret in the roof. Circular drive. Stable block. Somebody really rich must have lived in here once.

Marched up the snowy, unswept drive and pulled the bell. Heard it clang deep down inside the house.

Studying the blue and red tiles of the porch floor in the fading light when footsteps on other side of door, shuffling, like something out of Hammer House of Horror. Looked back over shoulder, but there was only the darkening drive.

Then the door opens a crack and this face peers out, permed hair sticking up like wires. Cheeks hung down in little sacks and when it spoke you expected the voice all rusty like the Tin Man. The sacks went up and down.

Old tweed skirt and hanging cardi. Slippers. God, she was a scruff.

Cleaner, thinks I, and said aloud, 'From the Job Centre. Come about the Nursing position.'

97

Also, 'Open sodding door, it's bloody freezing' – but not aloud.

She creaked it back a bit and I saw a little lobby with a wheelchair parked and crutches all in a heap. Then she said suspiciously, 'Ye'd better come in,' and I knew she was Scottish like the Glenlivet and our Roderick.

The lobby opened into a wide hall with an open fire with roaring flames. Leather armchairs either side and a polished drum table with a shining brass jug full of those tawny chrysanthemums, all very elegant and nice. Didn't go with the dotty old bat at all.

'Matron,' she says to me now and I blinked. But yes, when you looked there was a certain air of authority or perhaps the peevish look of someone wanting their own way.

Her little currant eyes gleamed above the cheek sacks as she looked at me. I'll swear she had forgotten I was coming.

'Come into ma office,' she cooed. 'Cold for the time of the year, is it not?'

Thought of saying, Often is in January, but breath taken by sight of that office. She laughed and pointed to the mess. 'I'm an industrious person, as you see.' Loada cow manure. There was books, papers, files . . . you name it, all around, and a monster big filing cabinet with open drawer she pushed with a bang, but not before you heard the clink of glass inside. What had little 'Reeny stumbled into?

'Do sit down,' she murmured, waving at old chair. 'Forgive the mess – it's working cayoss. Short-staffed at the moment. Illness, you know.'

'There's a lot of throats about,' I said politely, lowering the Purkiss bum. She sat down too, opposite, fished an old book and pencil out, licked it and looked at me. I give name and rank and service number as Stan says.

'Always cherished an ambition to become a nurse, have you?' she says fondly, cheek pouches up, up and away.

'No.'

'No? Come now!' she chided me. 'You're intelligent and articulate, I can see.'

I thought articulate was lorries.

'There's a uniform,' she says, dangle, dangle, dangle. 'It'll show off your waist.'

If I had one.

'And a ducky little blue and white cap.'

Well now, that did rather grab me. Thoughts of poncing about in front of Amy. Noreen Spink, SRN She'd have to put that on my birthday card envelopes.

Still, some remaining shreds of honesty made me say didn't know nothing about medicines, except Nasal Vic and what I picked up in commercials and Claire Rayner.

'You'll be instructed,' says the old bat.

'Trained?'

'Certainly.'

'Qualified?'

'Qualified for all sorts of things,' she said hurriedly. 'Will you have a cup of tea? I'll sort out a uniform to fit.'

I didn't fancy tea in that room. She bent down and rummaged in a tatty old box she had on the floor and came up all flushed and triumphant with something in a plastic bag.

A harassed nurse brought tea in on a tray I'd have been ashamed of. I took some just to please her.

'No cardigans underneath,' Matron Peebles said, her manner changing, getting harder. 'Hemline one inch below the knee. Cap must be starched. No slides, fancy combs or bows. No nail polish, lipstick or coloured stockings. You should wear black, lace-up, flat-heeled shoes at all times.'

Nearly asked her should I trim my bra. But she was offering £4 an hour.

Went out into the hall again, carrying plastic bag. The smell of lavender waxed furniture fairly hit you after the stale smell of her office. Had a vague feeling I'd been here before – I don't mean coming in. Deja view.

And with it was a feeling that hall just a beautiful, false facade. Hiding something.

'You can see the rooms tomorrow,' the old girl told me as if offering free food. 'There are three floors. I'll get Magwyn to show you round. I always place a new nurse under the wing of an experienced one. Till tomorrow, Nurse. Nine o'clock sharp.'

And with that she banged the door and I was left standing in the icy, snow-filled drive which someone still hadn't swept. It was dark now, too, and a harsh wind came moaning through the big trees. I was crazy for lights and warmth. Even her office seemed like paradise, looking back.

But I'd been called 'Nurse'.

'I just wish you'd told me,' Amy said in her soft voice. (Stopped off on way home.) 'Before you went, I mean. Down at the WVS that one's got a reputation for losing staff. Not a good person to work for.'

'Seems all right to me,' I said shortly. Wasn't having that from her. 'Give us a cup of tea. I'll show you my uniform.'

I fished it up out of the plastic bag all crumpled from cuddling it on the bus and held it up against me. Oh my God.

It was a blue striped dress, long and loose, baggy-saggy as Dorelia used to say about her gym knickers, far too big for me even though I am beginning to bulge a bit again. Felt plain silly there in front of Amy.

'Probably came out of store,' she said. 'I'll give you a hand with it. Just a second, while I put Suky on.'

I really ought to have gone home to him and the tea then, but that uniform I was ready to be so proud of made me want to cry. We took in giant darts, cut six inches off the hem and made wide seams in the sleeves and got it more or less to fit. But the cap was a limp, stupid affair, even with grips to hold it on. Amy

SprayRobined it and also gave me a black elastic belt she'd kept from way back in the 'Fifties.

I thought I looked quite smart. But then our Roderick came in.

'What's this badly made bed doing in here?' he asked.

Ignored him and asked Amy if she had any black stockings.

'Not 'alf,' said Roderick, straight-faced.

Amy blushed a bit and went to get them. The thought of her strutting her stuff for Roderick made me want to smile. It was me he used to be keen on that way.

Got pair low (*not* flat) shoes on way home. Buttons, not laces. Even so they depress me undeliably.

No replies to missing kitten ad. I put in Personal Column under *Lost and Found*. Thought of little animal lying under all this snow somewhere driving me nearly as barmy as those poxy shoes.

Came out of that place three minutes late today and missed bus home.

Old cow.

It was one of my Sue Lawley days and she hadn't liked that, had she. If you are a pouchy-faced, broad-beamed old bag you wouldn't. But I'd lost 4lb. and had my hair cropped and lightened with (few) grey hairs blended in at 'Sharp Business' and I was feeling chirpy. I was in three minutes late this morning from walking slowly on the icy bits, so what does she say but 'Right. You'll leave three minutes late this afternoon.'

Grange drive still not swept.

Lousy day anyway. Trouble with Cropper. Tired from lifting her about. Her head fell every which way.

Crappy Cropper, Magwyn calls her. We went in early to make her bed but she wouldn't get up at all. Kept asking us what day it was, over and over again until Magwyn shouted, 'Shut your gob!'

Got her into her chair at last and Magwyn yelled at her she could put her own clothes on today, she'd made us all behind.

We busy with bed, but she just sat there half naked, slyly playing with herself (she's lost most of her hair down there and all of her sense of shame), great white legs with bulging blue veins stuck out in front of her.

'Better get her dressed,' Magwyn says at last. 'Or we'll be here till Resurrection Day.'

Well of course she's messed her chair. Certain she does it just to annoy Magwyn, who can be sharp. Caught her watching Magwyn just like a naughty child.

'Shit!' said Magwyn, stating the obvious. 'You dirty old girl.'

Had to leave the room before I puked.

Cropper offered me some chocolate today. Pulled it out from under the bedclothes.

Turned to run out of room again and bumped against chest of drawers, knocking over photo in silver frame, Cropper forty year ago standing up straight and attractive in Wren uniform, medal ribbons on her chest. Stopped and replaced photo next to clock and Cropper roared at me to leave her things alone.

Nice little cleaner Pam who does the hall missing today. Thought she must be sick but Magwyn says had row with Peebles and stormed out.

'Happens all the time,' our Magwyn said. 'Wonder there's anyone left to run this bloody place.'

Dorelia gave me two books to read on the long bus ride.
AGELESS AGEING,
IN FAVOUR OF THE SENSITIVE MAN.

Took AGELESS to work with me today to read under table at morning coffee break. Breaks getting longer and longer because Peebles very, very, very slack. Some days slacker than others, knocking back cup after cup of black coffee with something Ivy (cook) puts in it from old Worcester Sauce bottle.

Kitchen coffee break forty-five minutes today, only ended when little Mr Ferguson, one of the ground floor residents, put his head round the door. Had the sense to flirt a bit with Matron saying he was missing her or I think she would have eaten him. Quite steady when she got down off her stool. I was amazed.

Told S. about the coffee breaks. Said, 'You get paid for it, don't you? Why grouse?'

Well yes, but that's no way to run a railroad.

Told Dorelia about The Grange.

She asked, 'What do the doctors make of it?'

I said, 'There aren't any doctors. Well not daily. All the old boys and girls are in single rooms. The posh ones open off the hall and the patients in them are all there and can chat nicely. Good but shabby live on the next floor and then there's really daft ones like Cropper on the second floor. Nobody sees them except the nurses.'

'No visitors?' she asked.

'Not encouraged,' I told her.

'Do you enjoy it?'

'Only the pay packet on a Friday afternoon,' I said. All the kudos of being a nurse had gone by the time of this conversation. Glorified bog attendant, me.

Fridays, there we all are, in the kitchen surrounded by the smell of stale cabbage with Peebles dishing the little packets out off a silver tray like sweeties. All saying 'Thank you, Matron,' one after the other.

Found out she actually lives right up there in the roof, over shop, over Cropper and all. A flat, she calls it, but Magwyn says just a collection of old rooms, servants' attics left from long ago. No one else is allowed up there. She comes down of a morning and goes back up there at night and if she's had a row with the Night Sister, all alone with her ancient loonies. Magwyn says she dopes 'em.

'Don't she ever go out?' I asked.

She shook her head. 'Never leaves the place. Even has her shopping delivered.'

Peebles gives me the creeps. But for £140 a week, anyone can do that.

Amy called to say Fella bit Eamonn. He now issuing ultimatum to the McKays – either he goes or the dog. Amy in state. I said surely no contest. Chuck him out!

He's at home afternoons now. Asked him to do things like peel potatoes for when I get in. We got square spuds.

Gets shopping, though, if I leave list, and will even go to launderette if put in large blue plastic bag with handles, the one down Elmers End, of course, by 'SteamPast'.

Maybe I was wrong. *Says* all he wants is bits for his trains. Coming to fetch me in the car these days, dead on five, never late. Says if I'm kept, going to come in and sort la Peebles out.

Yes, well.

Came skidding into drive (still not swept) early today. Peebles and me in Sluice. She say, 'Who dat?' I said, 'My husband.'

'Thought you was a widow,' she says indignantly. 'You told me you was widowed in the War.'

'Not old enough,' I told her. 'I was only six when it ended.'

'Someone's mixed up,' she says, giving me a sharp look.

'Tisn't me. Maybe Ivy should stick Gumment Health Warning on Worcester Sauce bot.

Panic. Notification Inspectors coming fortnight's time.

Peebles on phone to decorators urgent, pep talk to Staff, harassment of inmates. Doddering about and asking daft questions now forbidden.

Magwyn gets over-keen, shouts at little Ferguson. I found him crying in the toilet like a baby. Gave him a cuddle.

New menus (well, old food writ posh) thought up and Ivy grumbles at having to letter it all out and stick it up in communal place. Where she'd like to stick it, another matter and not quite nice. Also, she's so used to blending everything into one grey tasteless mash on account of old things having few teeth she doesn't want to set food out properly on plates. Even mixes pastry, rhubarb and custard in blender so it comes out dog's muck brown. Cropper loves that, of course. Holds plate up and head back so the mess just dribbles into her mouth and all around. (Can't see, myself, why Ivy doesn't do greens and rhubarb, potatoes, gravy, meat and custard all in one, but she will insist on having the courses traditional separate.)

Now, Nurses will have to spoon-feed.

'Shan't bloody do it,' is Magwyn's answer to that one.

Painters arrive and almost immediately chat up Magwyn. Thought she'd take um but see she's got more and more buttons undone every time she passes man up a ladder.

Went into Sluice a bit quick this afternoon and come on Magwyn kneeling in front of one of the decorators giving him a mouth job through the opening in his overalls. He was bucking about and enjoying himself so much he never noticed me. Then he began to groan, holding her each side of her head, completely out of his mind, and I backed out tootsweet.

Stood outside in the corridor like a lemon with three warm, full bedpans in my hands worrying Peebles would turn up.

After a bit they came out. Magwyn looked to me as if she'd had a treat too, and winked.

Later, doing Mrs Zenoni-Vail next door to Cropper, asked her wasn't she afraid of catching AIDS. She said, it was quite all right, she used to be engaged to that particular painter.

'Not going to get it off of someone you know, are you?' she said.

Had never really realized it was as simple as just that.

Panic again. Zenoni-Vail trailed her fingers along a freshly painted wall, leaving four wobbly grooves and leopard spots here and there. How Magwyn laughed.

'Can't wait till she sees it,' she said.

'Better get your ex to tart it up,' I told her.

Peebles has Scotch fit like Roderick when she sees and goes off to find painters, now in Laundry, and rubs them up the wrong way so that Magwyn's ex says no can do again. Helps herself liberally to Worcester after, so that in fifty minute break which follows, sways slightly on her stool.

Even her office has a pansy-out. Should think local bottle banks very, very grateful.

'Amy all right, is she?' he asked me at breakfast this morning. 'Coping?'

''Course she's coping,' I told him. 'Amy hasn't got a job.'

'Don't mean she don't work,' he said.

'Means she can please herself whether she makes pastry, walks the dog or paints by numbers,' I said tersely. 'Anyway, you were the one who didn't want him here. Said you didn't like the smell.'

Called in at Amy's on the way home.

Eamonn in bed when I got there.

'Passed out?' I asked. 'Or Fella bitten him again?'

'Chickenpox,' Amy said. 'Picked it up Cator Park,

106

helping me do Meals on Wheels a fortnight ago. There was a spotty little boy visiting his grandpa. When he's better Roddy's got plans to dry him out completely.'

Speechless. Patted Fella's head without realizing and rubbed his ears. He doesn't rate me very highly. Amy's dog.

'That's terrific,' I said at last. 'You're both wonderful. Hope it doesn't cost you.'

She made me a cup of tea and broke open a slab of chocolate.

'You're all right, then?' I said.

'Oh yes.'

'Not too tired.'

'No.'

'Fine. That's just fine,' I said. 'I've got this friend at work, see, too tired for . . . Well, anyrate, she doesn't *feel* like it so much these days.'

'Go on,' she says, bending down to get potatoes out of the veg. rack. She put them in a bowl in the sink and ran water on them.

'Her husband's very demanding. She said to me, '"Reen, whatever do you do? Can't keep pretending I've got 'eadache.'' Well, I didn't know what to say. I mean, hardly my problem.'

'Does your friend feel she can't talk to her husband?'

'Well yes,' I said. 'That's about the size of it.'

'Perhaps she's really fond of him and doesn't want to hurt his feelings?'

'No, she doesn't.'

'But if she refuses him she's frightened he may look elsewhere?'

'Yeah,' I said, thinking of the train shop girl.

'Perhaps she feels she knows him all too well – the way he leaves his socks on the floor and how the hairs grow out of his ears.'

'And the way he farts in bed,' I said with feeling. 'I think my friend mentioned that 'n' all.'

107

'Then there's your trouble,' the RELATE counsellor said. 'They've grown too used to each other. Too much like old pals.'

'Meaning you don't fuck your friends?' I held out my teacup for a refill. 'Now that's a thought. Not too much milk. So what would you advise me to tell her, my friend at work?'

'Fantasize,' Amy said. 'Close your eyes and pretend he's Charles Dance or something.'

'I don't rate Charles Dance at all,' I said. 'Never have fancied fair blokes.'

'Well someone from the old days, then. You used to like Gregory Peck.'

'And James Mason and Stewart Granger.'

'Yes. Pretend you're at a gang-bang with a load of Stewart Grangers.'

'That's what you'd tell my friend to do?'

'Oh yes,' Amy said. She put two large peeled potatoes on a chopping board and started to make chips. Upstairs a floorboard creaked. We both looked up at the ceiling.

'I'll just go and see if he wants anything,' she said, and went out, smiling, God knows why. Chickenpox isn't that funny.

Didn't go up and see Eamonn. *Think* I've had it, but it's best to be sure.

Picked up rest of chocolate slab and left for home.

He didn't go up to his trains this evening. Watched an old episode of *Minder*.

Me watching him watching it.

Half past ten, he made Ovaltine.

'Remember when we used to both bath together?' I asked him, and he looked up, surprised.

'That was one hell of a time ago.'

'How about joining me, then?'

'Leave it out, 'Reen,' he said. 'We'd never both get in. Well, not us and water too.'

Went up, bathed and sprayed myself heavily with the White Satin. Then put on summer nightie, one with straps. *Cleavage.*

'Won't you be cold?' was all he said when he come up.

Lay there. Wasn't going to start anything. Thought of Anthony Valentine.

'What you looking so smug about?' he asked. 'Why you lying there with your eyes shut, grinning?'

'Free country,' I said.

He grunted and snuggled down. Let him have stone pig.

He is – they are locked together in a timeless embrace while his lips take hers hungrily as if he can never have enough demanding with a passionate intensity that sets her trembling as though he would draw her very soul up through her eyes and she clings to him as the one stable thing in a shifting world while his strong hands crush the filmy stuff of her robe making her feel the male hardness of . . .

. . . his thighs, because of course it's Stanley Spink, eager and thrusting, though if you keep your eyes shut it could be Clark Gable, Tyrone Power, Laurence Olivier, George Sanders, Marlon Brando, Laurence Harvey, Trevor Howard, Herbert Lom . . .

. . . wearing socks for the cold, of course.

Told him at breakfast I was going to buy electric blanket.

Sunday. Still no answer to kitten ad. Have put additional pcs in PO window, drycleaner's, Safeways', and on our front garden gate.

Up Duck lunchtime with Wayne and Dorelia. Stan chuffed because kids wanted to come with us.

'You spend twenty years growing them up,' he often says moodily. 'Then just when they're starting to turn out right and you're beginning to see what you've got they get stuck in elsewhere.'

'You make 'em sound like row of carrots on allotment,' I told him.

Still, it was pleasant to have them along, though there were flies in this nice ointment.

There was this Yorkshireman in the pub, a builder, Alf, mostly mouth, a real goop. Know him by sight, that's all and quite enough. Why Dora lets him in, she being a feminist, I'll never know.

This charmer eyed me and Dorelia giggling together. I could see him watching and he didn't like it. He tried to muscle in on Stan and Wayne but they weren't having any. Then suddenly the stunted yokel rounds on me.

'Hast tha got his dinner in t'oven?'

Just for a minute there couldn't see the sense. Slow. Then I smiled the way you do at iffy jokes. And then it hit me even if it was a joke, none of his damn business. Didn't suss though, at the time, that what he really meant was I should be at home.

I had a decent upbringing. I just stared. Dorelia said, 'How about minding your own business?' but Wayne, who only heard the last part of what Alf said, whirled round, thinking man making apropos observations on his wife.

Wayne's got 'ot temper. Plenty of ironware too, on his chest amongst all the curling hair, St Christopher, Pisces the Fish in silverguilt, George and the Dragon and all. On another man this might look ephemeral, but Wayne is no wimp, even if he does read Ted Hughes. In a flash, up beside Yorkshire on his stool.

'Anything to say, you say it to me,' he says, breathing. His medals clanged and Alf for the first time looked a bit doubtful.

'I only asked . . .'

'We heard, sweedeart,' said Wayne, lip curling like Clint Eastwood in *Dirty Harry*, ladida teaching accent flown clean away.

'Don't make a fuss,' his father-in-law puts in (charming)

and Wayne swings round on him, metal bits clinking.

'I don't like oiks in pubs.' Then to Alf – 'Push off, dickhead. And don't let me ever catch you doing that again.'

Look on the bright side, Alfie. It could have been detention or a hundred lines. Muttering, he slid off his stool and went out, banging the door.

Didn't dare tell Wayne he was really talking to me.

S. got another round and told some of his old, familiar jokes from way back when, laughing too loudly.

Drives me wild.

Extra Sunday barmaid in miniskirt then give him diversion.

'I *like* thighs,' he murmured into his beer.

'No one would ever have guessed,' I reassured him.

Time to go. Known him, man and dogsbody, over thirty years and when he starts babbling about thighs it's time to get him home.

Climbing carefully down off my stool (they're making them for rabbit arses these days) when caught him goggling across at straw-haired bimbo in ohmygod microskirt; long, long boots and Madonna gloves on her hands.

'Get him out,' I said to Wayne. 'Get your father-in-law out of here!'

He looked at me but he took Stan's arm. S. let himself be trotted along, looking back over his shoulder all the time like a child dragged away from a circus. Waved at the bimbo, calling out, 'Ta-ta!'

'See you!' she shouted, blowing him a kiss and looked at me with message of Get This.

Might have guessed then and there who she was but wasn't going to let myself think anything yet. We got Stan out and stood him on the pavement. And from behind us came this voice.

'Got new rolling stock if you want to come in Thursday!'

Should have thought the whole street heard.

So that was her.

That was what all the fuss was about.

Up to now I hadn't put a face to her so she hadn't really existed. But now I felt stripped somehow, face to face with reality. And that cold wind was back again and blowing all around me.

Too much.

Dorelia put a hand under my arm, but I couldn't bear her pity and I pulled away. Afterwards I felt bad because it was Baby, but I couldn't help it, not at the time.

We got home and I did Sunday dinner, a roast; beef with horse radish sauce and little peas and colly and crispy potatoes, all bleeding and half raw the way he likes it.

Then men wanted to watch old film, *The Gun*, with Sophia Loren and cans of beer and crisps out of the fridge. I went out to the kitchen to make scones and put salt instead of sugar in.

They went about four. He said, 'You're quiet.'

'Wishing I looked like that Sophia Loren.'

He said, 'Most of it's false, you bet. Anyway, she's married to some fat old geezer.'

Ain't we all?

Went upstairs and washed my hair and gave myself a cucumber facial. Then I had a bath, shaved my legs and took off all my old chipped varnish and painted them bright red, the way you do for summer. Then I put on a clean housecoat and went down.

He said, 'Going up the pub again, don't mind, do you? See you're all ready for bed.'

That cold wind began to blow again, more strongly.

'But you never go up Sunday night,' I whispered.

'Yeah, well,' he said. 'Something to sort out.'

'Got money to fling around, then?'

'Oh, for Pete's sake!' he said irritably. 'I'll only have half a pint.'

When he'd gone, finished off the crisps and beer.

Kittens, what's left of them, growing fast. Book I got from Miss Sweetbush says to have five small meals a day. But with me working I can only give them three. One of them can lap.

Found DON'T LOOK ROUND!!! down settee and remembered I had vowed to follow its advice always.

Took three sticks celery for lunch. Magwyn rude.

Out in lunch hour (Peebles don't like that at all) to 'Naughty Girls' in Beckenham Road and bought black peep-thru bra, seam stockings and suspenders. Bra really too small but don't matter as tips meant to show.

And do. Look a bit like Swiss Alps sticking out when walk. The hills are alive!

Back a little late but she didn't notice. Standing staring at letter in her hand, must have come by lunch time post.

Place in rare old state around her; Ivy blaspheming, others flustered.

Thinking about problems so much, had forgotten the Inspectors.

Kittens getting round, Wayne says globular. Look like little Easter Eggs on sticks. Eating scrambled egg, minced beef, hashed up fish bits, tinned and frozen prawns, a little bran to keep them regular, chopped sprouts and brewer's yeast and sprinklings from his Alpen.

He said, 'Everything gets fat in this house.'

Gloomy.

No good cleaning Cropper up. She'd only do it all over again for their benefit. Has unexhaustible supply from all that blended goo, but beats me how.

Peebles screeching at us why hasn't she been done? (Cropper.) So me and Magwyn did her and made her dress. Asked, 'What day is it, darling?' And Magwyn said, 'Not going to tell you unless you pull your knickers up.'

So the old girl pulled them up tootsweet and looked all hopeful up at Magwyn and Magwyn went out of the room without telling her.

Mean.

Took her tea in at eleven and she asked again.

'If you drink your tea I'll tell you,' I said and she drank it up quick and looked up just like a baby.

'It's Tuesday,' I said.

'Tuesday,' she said. 'Thank you, darling. Tuesday, Tuesday, Tuesday, Tuesday, Tuesday. What day did you say it was?'

Thought of saying, 'Tell you if you promise not to poo in your chair,' but then realized she'd forget she'd promised.

'I seen them,' Magwyn said to me in the corridor. 'Miserable bunch of farts in dark suits. Look like Russians. She got her posh voice on.'

They lunched in the Residents' Lounge (no Residents allowed). Saw all round. God knows what they made of the Laundry.

Drove off in cars about four thirty, leaving Peebles weak. Worcester Sauce. Long, long kitchen break. She smoked.

Later me and Mags went into Laundry with sheets just to talk and while I shoved it into long lines of rusting automatics she made a coffee. Dropped a mug on the stone floor, fortunately empty, but Peebles must have heard crash and came hurrying in just as Magwyn picking up pieces and I put coffee jar in empty machine.

She say, 'What that kettle for?'

'Dissolving Biotex,' Magwyn told her.

Suspicious, darting eyes all over, cheek pouches up and down, up and down.

'Blimey, wouldn't want her nerves,' Magwyn said

(when she was gone). 'What's she got to hide?'

'All over now anyway,' I said, retrieving coffee.

'Ye-es,' Magwyn said. 'You know, I wouldn't half like to see up in her flat.'

Went up to bed early. Put on new bra and then suspenders, seam stockings. When he came up couldn't help seeing, but looked all embarrassed.

'Very nice, 'Reen,' he said, getting into bed and rolling over, back to me.

Felt a right wally.

Kicked off high heels I was wearing and got into bed. Felt funny without my nightie.

''Night, 'Reen,' he said, still with his back to me.

Don't think I ever felt so humiliated. Lay there and listened to him snoring and tears come and I fought them off and my nose got blocked and I sat up and blew and it come out like a trumpet call but he didn't hear.

Suspenders had buttons that dug in and hurt. Leaned down and undid the bloody things and threw them out.

In the morning kicked them under the bed in rage. Kittens found them and played tug-o'-war.

Carrying trouble to work like cloud of flies round head. Magwyn asked what was up and like a fool I told her. Now it'll get all round.

Still, she was nice and told me about her first, who used to tie her to the bed and then dress up as harem eunuch come to perform female circumcision.

I said, 'They don't really do that, do they?'

'He said all nice ones do.'

'What about the naughties?'

'They get left to play with themselves. He used to use little white plastic knives he'd saved from a holiday plane flight.'

I wanted to hear more but just then Peebles stuck her face round Sluice door to say she weren't running rest home for nurses.

Magwyn told me she run off with a bookie at sixteen. After that she had a grave-digger down Woodside and after that a milkman lived in Sundridge Park. Then AIDS and HIV and things come up and she slowed down. Now she got steady man on dole, supporting him.

'I gotta keep this job,' she sighed. 'He's really nice. Though after Bob the Book none of them was ever into pain. I'd give anything sometimes if he'd only rough me up a bit.'

'Don't talk so daft,' I told her.

But she sighed again. 'Shows they care.'

'You don't know what you're talking about,' I said. 'That's bloody stupid.'

'Better'n turning his back on you in bed,' she said.

Later, coming away from taking in little Ferguson's lunch I happened to look up the stairs.

Two people were standing up there where the staircase bends; one was a tall, good-looking man with fair hair tied back on his neck, long tail coat and breeches, polished boots. She wore a flowing dress with skirts and she hung on his arm and looked up at him and you would have thought nothing in the world existed for her but him.

She adored him. Can't write how happy she seemed. They were about to be married, though don't ask how I knew that.

What stood out was she was over the moon with joy. It sort of glowed in her face. She was shy and yet eager and somehow just plain glad he was going to use her body . . .

All so different from what you hear today. Me, I never felt like that about a man in all my life. How can you adore summing you can see through always?

Felt like intruder and turned away. When I looked back they'd gone.

Shrugged and got on with Cropper's goo. Pancakes and

lemon and blancmange. Ivy had got it sort of junk yard grey.

Didn't occur to me till later to ask someone what those two were doing up there in *fancy dress*. So full of own thoughts, that particular blip just didn't cross my screen.

Weekend. Telly lousy. Slush in streets, brown and grey like cooking at The Grange. Aurora North-Brightley has lost her grip. Shall write to her, care of her publishers.
    I am fat, fat, fat, fat, fat.
    What did I say I was, Miss Cropper?

Moved Plum and family downstairs and firmly shut bedroom door. Too many antics in the night. Thump, bump of kittens playing merrily. Also means a toilet tray up there.
    Too much.
    S. nailed hardboard cover over little door to make sure she don't get pregnant again.

If only something I could bloody do, but can't even mention it to him. Tried, but he just turns away all awkward.
    'Are they having it off?' Dorelia repeated when I went round there Sat. Well, had to speak to somebody. Desperate. Wasn't talking to Amy again. Feel sure she knew it was me and not a friend at work last time. Anyway, she and everybody else can see my cloud of flies.
    'If you ask me, the answer's no,' my child went on. 'Daddy wouldn't.'
    Well, she would say that.
    'He's human,' I reminded her. Well, so he is. Almost.
    'You know . . .' she said.
    'Get on with it.'
    'Mum, don't get this wrong. But you always sort of put him down.'
    'Whose side you on?'
    'Both your sides. I just want to see you happy again

together, like you used to be. All this business is a recent thing, isn't it?'

Couldn't tell her he's been cack-handed in bed for years and bloody years. Couldn't tell her he wasn't like in Charlotte Lamb and dear Aurora.

But then, is any man? Isn't their trouble they are Real Life? I mean, you never hear afterbirth mentioned in Georgette Heyer.

She laughed. 'Daddy will have to be masterful,' she said. 'Don't be hard on him. I think all men are screw-centered and not really very imaginative, that's what it comes to.'

I'd no business loading Baby with my affairs, especially a grouse against her Dad.

'Just a patch we're going through.' I said, probably too late. 'We'll get over it.'

'Men have some funny ways,' she said. 'And talking of funny, it's strange to think Daddy is a man.'

'Matter for debate,' I said darkly, and got up to go. She give me a hug and a kiss as well as she could for the baby. 'Still, look on the bright side, eh? At least we got our health.'

But oh, how wrong can you be?

Prognostication is the thief of time, my old mother used to tell me when I was young so when I was back I didn't dally but got down to cleaning the house and when he come in (God knows where he been, he didn't say) I tackled him head on. Thought Dorelia's right. Talk to him, girl. Then there won't be bogeys hiding in the cupboards, they'll be out.

Aimed to be tactful, subtle-like and delicate.

Still things don't always work out like they should.

Said, 'You haven't felt much like it lately. Wasser matter – it dropped off or summing?'

He jumped so much he rattled his teacup and spoon.

'I been meaning to talk to you, 'Reen,' he said after a bit, stirring his tea and staring at it for strength.

118

There was a pause and then that old, cold wind began to lift and stir and blow. Here comes the end of *Semper Idem*, I thought. No Grandad for the little girl, or perhaps he'll visit her with his popsy. Granny all by herself in council flat.

I was alone in the world.

I might fall off the edge.

'I got a bit of trouble,' he said. 'Down below.'

'Down below?'

He nodded, a bit ashamed. Things aren't supposed to be less than perfect there.

(Though of course, as Wayne once pointed out to me in The Duck after four pints, the future of the human race depends on *them*. It ain't woman's ability to conceive that matters, it's man's ability to get it up.)

'Seen anyone about it?' I started to say and then clean forgot all words as a huge thought came thundering: He's not knocking off the train shop girl. Can't be. Alleluia, praise de Lord. His poker's gone all wrong.

'Wayne,' he said. 'Only him. I went back to the pub Sunday. You remember. He said he'd meet me there.'

And supposing he and Dorelia swapped notes, as they're bound to do?

'You never!' I exclaimed, annoyed.

'Well, I did,' he said.

'All right. What did he say?'

'See the doctor. Said it sounded like cystitis, but he couldn't be sure. Might be pros something.'

'Did you?'

'No.'

'Daft monkey. You haven't been putting it about?'

'How could I?' he asked savagely. 'I couldn't even if I wanted to.'

I put an arm round him and he clutched me hard, burying his face.

'Mog, you got a lovely chest,' he said, his voice all

119

muffled. 'You don't want to lose it. You come off that poxy little diet, you hear?

'I been feeling so rotten and didn't like to tell you,' he went on. 'And you got all new gear, just for me, I saw and I couldn't do anything and I thought Oh, *shit*!' He held me hard and his hand went up the back of my legs.

'*There!*' he said suddenly and bitterly, opening his own legs, looking down. 'Nothing moving at all.'

'Can't do if it hurts.' I pointed out. 'Stands to reason.'

'That's just what it don't do,' he said gloomily.

'I got some stuff,' I said, remembering. It was something Dorelia left behind, though I didn't tell him that. It was for 'honeymoon cystitis', what you get if you go it too long and hard. She left it along with her guitar.

I got it and made him drink some. Mist. Pot. Cit. I had some too in case the thing was catching.

Then we both went up to bed and I slept as I hadn't slept for days.

Went out in lunch hour and bought these little jars for celery, pickled onions, beetroot and so on, all in the shape of what goes in them. I do like to have things right and left to himself at home in the afternoons, S. will put sugar in the sago jar. Now even he will be able to get things right.

Peebles saw me go. When I got back I made a little display of them on the lunch table in that smelly old kitchen and said, 'Look, Matron, don't you think these are cute?'

Of course she had to say Yes, especially with Vera, Ivy and the rest going Ooh and Aah.

There's no law, Wayne says, states that you can't go out in lunch hours. It's just that Peebles doesn't like it. But you can't keep a freedom-loving Purkiss down.

He's been to doctor's. Was asked if he'd mind seeing Dr Bennett, the lady, and he took fright and nearly left

120

town. I said just a doctor like a man only a woman, and he said that's the trouble.

'She might have wanted to see it,' he said.

Told him he should be so lucky.

'How many you showed it to recently?' I asked. Then I remembered.

'Only Sharon down the train shop,' he said slyly.

I said, 'That's not funny!'

'Do you think I'd joke about it if it was true?'

I don't know.

'Still hurt?' I asked.

'When I go. Agony. Most of the time, though, just sort of aches.'

'Making you remember you got one?'

'Never really thought I hadn't. What is this, anyway? You didn't really think what Wayne said Dorelia said you thought?'

I turned away without replying.

'Moggy, you daft thing,' he said.

'Well, you were always down there.'

'Yeah, after trains.'

'So you say.'

'Oh well. Cuppa tea?'

'If you wouldn't rather go down the train shop.'

'Oh pack it in!' he said. 'Joke's over.'

Pain making him bad-tempered, I regret to say.

When we were up, he stooped and picked something off the bedroom floor.

A suspender.

'You really going back into stockings, then,' he asked, all eagerness.

'Well, I bought some.'

'Got 'em on?'

'No, I give 'em to the cats to play with.'

He thought it was sarcasm. Then looked as if I was barmy.

'Shouldn't give them to the cats,' he said at last. 'The little ones might swallow them.'

Got into bed and held on to each other spoons. Then his voice come somewhere by my right ear.

'You really gonna wear suspenders, 'Reen?'

'If I can find them again.'

'Strewf,' he said. 'It's hurting. Almost wish you hadn't told me. We won't look now, but Moggy, I think it's moving.'

Countess not well. Called S. to say thinks it's her heart. He over there all day Sat. She kept him busy, oh yeah.

Rain, rain, nothing but bloody rain.

Two Valentine cards, though. One enormous with huge blue elephant with goo-goo eyes. And judging by way he smirked at breakfast, from him.

Other one had UNKNOWN ADMIRER in big wobbly letters inside.

Pleased.

Took to work and flashed them in front of the girls.

Magwyn said, 'Must be a real treat at your age.'

Little bitch.

At morning coffee Matron announces unpresidented news. Going out today. To Bromley to see her solicitor. Means she'll be away whole of the afternoon.

Happiness in kitchen. Then Vera, silly cow, has to ask, 'What time do you hope to get back, Matron?'

Immediately suspicions are aroused.

'About five,' she answers, little piggy eyes glinting in hope of catching us trying to piss off early.

Watched her drive off in taxi and Magwyn said, 'At least we'll know when she comes back. You can't mistake that taxi-engine noise.' She winked at me. 'We'll take a little look at her flat. Wait till I give the word.'

Did Cropper and the old dame next to her, Mrs Zenoni-Vail, who insists on wearing lipstick all the time and getting it all over her pillow. Cropper wanted to go back to bed, so we let her. Then we did downstairs for a bit then we snuck up craftily to the attic floor, making sure nobody saw us go.

Dead quiet up there. I was – well, not scared exactly, but something. We tried her door. It was locked.

Magwyn took out a hairgrip and fiddled with the lock and presently it gave. The door swung open and the rooms just lifted their eyes and looked at us.

It was awful. There was such a feel of her about. There was a kitchen and a bedroom and a bathroom all done up ever so nicely and full of the old girl's things. I didn't like it. I thought, Be glad when this is over.

'Here, look at this,' said Magwyn. Shelves and shelves and shelves of china, mostly blue and white, with pictures. She picked up a vase.

'For God's sake put it down,' I told her but she just turned it over.

'Delft,' she said and shrugged and put it back. Then she picked up a soup tureen, must have been part of an old dinner service once, big and chunky, very nice if you like that kind of thing. The blue of the pattern was bleeding out into the white.

'Dav-en-port,' read Magwyn.

Then she lost interest and went over to the window.

'Here's that funny tower thing,' she said, craning to see up on to the roof. The window was a bay, sort of round box in shape, plenty of room for two. I went to look. The turret didn't seem to be part of the flat.

'Always wanted a bedroom in one of those when I was a kid,' Magwyn said. 'She hasn't half got a lot of nice things, though. Look at that Chinese cabinet and those rugs hanging on the wall. She's worf a few quidlies.'

Then that naughty girl started going through Peebles' things, all her little drawers and stuff, and the writing desk with pigeon holes. She took down books and opened up a sewing box and went through the dressing table in the bedroom. She didn't take anything, just looked, as far as I could see, but I began to wish we hadn't come. I felt bad.

'Relax,' our Magwyn said. 'She's in Bromley, remember? Still, we'll go back now. The others'll wonder where we are, and 'sides, I seen enough.'

But she dallied over by the window.

''Ere!' I heard her call suddenly. 'There's someone in the . . .'

That girl was frozen to the spot when I looked round. Staring out across the roof.

'Oh, dear Christ . . .' I heard her whisper.

Then she stumbled out of that bay, hands held out before her.

'Outa here, quick!'

'Who . . . ?' I asked, but I already knew. The answer was in her face.

'Bloody, stinking Matron,' she said, blundering into a large china elephant which stood by a chair. 'Shift your arse, 'Reen!'

Ran for the stairs. Of course the front door wouldn't shut behind us properly so we left it any old how and hurtled down to Cropper's. Poor old Cropper was asleep.

'Quick, be changing her,' Magwyn said and we bundled Cropper upright, all blinking and nodding that huge head of hers and asking what day it was. The sheets were warm and damp and foul, which was good for once and we rip them off while listening for footsteps at the door.

'Go slow,' I said, when we had them on the floor. 'And don't breathe like that. She'll know we been running.'

But it was 'orrible trying to get your breath in that room with old Cropper in it. Magwyn dumped two pillows on Cropper's lap in the chair, stood up and said, 'Open the window for Gawd's sake, 'Reen.'

I said, 'Hang on a minute. *How can she be back?* I didn't hear no taxi or anything.'

Went to the door and opened it a crack. Calm enough outside. The upstairs hall, a sort of common room, was full of old dears slumped in chairs. Lipstick-Vail was reading *The Times* and Fergy had a little glass of Guiness.

'You *sure* you saw her?' I asked, turning back to Magwyn.

'As God is my witness,' she said.

'But what was she doing?'

'Nuffing. That's what's so bad. Stood there with her arms folded, just *looking* . . .' Magwyn put her hands over her eyes. 'God, it was awful.'

I believed her. We changed Cropper and dressed her, dawdling as we did so, answering her questions and being patient when she got her toes stuck in her tights. She must have thought Heaven had come right down.

'Thank you, darlings,' the old thing said, nodding and blowing off delicately in her chair.

'Anything else you want?' Magwyn asked and then, crossing to stand over by the chest of drawers, 'Blimey, you weren't half a looker once.'

We were scared to go down to the kitchen for lunch, but it was twelve now by Cropper's clock and we were more scared to stay here. In the end we went down, into the smell of ancient cabbage.

Ivy said, 'You're early. Lay the table.' And when we looked at kitchen clock it was only 11.45, just enough time for her to walk in and catch us on our own.

Magwyn said chirpily, 'Clock's wrong. I'll alter it.'

Ivy said, 'Leave it. I'm timing veg.'

'Any sign of Peebles yet?' Magwyn asked casual.

''Course not!' Ivy snapped, dishing up in great clouds of steam at one of the sinks.

Couldn't eat. But had lovely thought and wondered if Magwyn had had it too, only for her it wouldn't be so nice: *Only she'd been seen at the window.* Comforting.

She didn't come and she didn't come. Looked at Magwyn and wondered if she'd tell on me – that I was up there too and decided she wouldn't.

Rotten slimy tart and ice cream for afters.

Still she didn't come.

About four o'clock a taxi drew up on the drive and spat Peebles out into the rain. Saw it out of Sluice window.

Told Magwyn. She say impossible, she saw what she saw.

Got very busy with medicine trolley early for afternoon round, hands so wet and trembling could hardly grasp bar.

She came in through front hall down below, looked up, saw me and nodded, quite pleasantly for her, and then disappeared into her office. Little drinkie-poo, as Larch Mulliner would have said. Could have done with one myself.

'Well, 'Reen,' Magwyn said with that old dark Welsh directness of hers, 'if it wasn't her up at the window, it was her ghost. I seen her. So – if she was in Bromley all this time, who the hell was it up in the bloody tower?'

Search me. We look at each other for a long, long time. And then we turn away.

Saturday. Took him shopping. Spring in the air. Shops full of daffodils and latest autumn fashions. Went in all the chemists and tried perfume testers. Then tried to share my thoughts with him.

Had a copy of IN FAVOUR OF THE SENSITIVE MAN in my bag.

Sat on a bench in Crystal Palace District Cemetery. Told him about Sylvia Plath. Then about Simone de Beauvoir. Then about Joan Didion.

He said rather have Joan Collins, par for the course.

I said, 'The sensitive man is aware of woman's needs. He seeks to let her be.'

He said, 'You let me be. Gotta get out of the Pay and Display.'

I said, 'In IFOTSM we read that women need an inner laboratory of the soul, a world from which we can draw wisdom and our lucidities.'

He said, 'Don't mean you have to go round smelling like old whore's handbag, does it?'

And I cried, 'Oo-oo-ooh! Gimme THE SENSITIVE MAN!'

And hit him over the head with it.

Who is this Sylvia Plath?

D. said, 'A poet. She's been dead some years.'

'Out of date, then?' I said. 'What you gimme out-of-date stuff for?'

'Because she's relevant.'

'What's this relevant?'

'She was in the van of the Women's Movement decades ago. She did her own thing.'

I said so did Elizabeth I.

That set her back a bit. I was pleased. Not often you get the better of your educated daughter. And I've always admired Queen Elizabeth I, in a general sort of way. For that matter I've always admired Marie Helvin and Jerry Hall. Point I'm making is you don't have to be no feminist.

I've always got right in there and mixed it and (usually) got what I wanted anyway.

Asked how I was getting on with AGELESS AGEING. I said fine, making her father take brewer's yeast on his Alpen. Also told her it cleared up his little trouble, we both swear by it now.

Wayne thought very funny (in The Mucky Duck, Sun. lunch time). Said brewer's yeast called for incantation of some kind.

'Up, Stan, up. Arise and smile.
Take a crap and shave the dial.'

I said, 'More likely

"Cough and fart, cough and fart,
That's the way that mornings start."

All laughed, but it wasn't very good for Stan's moral.
    No sign of Sharon Trainshop.

What didn't tell D. was that S. said wasn't spending five
quid on fancy, ladida pills as recommended by Ms
Kenton (author) for me or any other, be she the Queen of
Sheba. Or that, looking at her pretty photo on the jacket,
said, 'Why has this tart got her head all on one side?'
Didn't want to upset Dorelia.

Another phone call from the Countess. Wish she'd just
pack up and go. S. over to dance attendance as usual
Sat. and Sun. *But she isn't ill.* Just wants attention. All
another false facade.

Sacked. Magwyn grassed on me, conniving, rotten little
bitch.
    It started with me asking Ivy who's been there for ever
if there was someone living secretly upstairs. She gimme
loadsbunny about ghosts.
    Then Magwyn comes up and tells us she's seen a letter
from this Bromley solicitor to Peebles, which mentioned
Allowances for certain old people – Residents, which
had cheques attached.
    'You mean financial ones?' I asked. 'She's getting paid
to give them extras?'
    'Yep.'
    'I never seen any extras.'
    'Oh yes you have,' says Magwyn. 'They're blue and
they're white and they're called Delft and Davenport.'
    Told Stan about all this but he just laughed and said
we'd never prove a thing.
    But I think we should try. Maybe write to Esther
Ranzten or something. *Something.*

Said to Magwyn thought we should confront her.

'What – tell her we been up there?' she cried, real fright in her eyes. 'Noway! Not this little girl. I need this job.'

'Think of poor old Cropper,' I said. 'That's no life, bed to chair and back to bed again.'

'How's telling Peebles going to help?'

'It might.'

'No, no!' she said in alarm. 'You just leave it, 'Reen. You promise me.'

But I wouldn't promise her, would I, and I went home and come back the next day full of what Wayne calls a crusading spirit. Only to find that Magwyn has got in there before me and told Peebles it was me that broke the china elephant.

Didn't even know it had been broken.

Tried to tell Peebles I hadn't been alone but it was all too much like Infants' School and ya, ya, I'll get you. Anyway, she wouldn't believe me. Just looking for excuse to gimme cards. Had it in for me ever since I swanned off lunch hours. So I come home furious and nearly tearful.

Stanley really, really nice and lovely. All for going round there seeing her. Wayne said sue the bag. Wrongful dismissal.

'Don't matter,' I said wearily. 'Only tuppeny-ha'pny job and anyway I was getting tired of it. Dettol up your nose all the time.'

And it may have been only 2½d. job, but here's goodbye to my new Dolphin Luxury Bathroom Accessories (gold or chrome-plated) with fixing screws, Littlewoods M.O. Also solid wood mahogany-finish Olde Worlde toilet seat, £39.99, (scrub with Domestos) that I'd had in mind since reading new spring catalogue.

Shit.

S. to see his mother. Asked on return whether we ought

to have her live with us, she was so poorly.

Speechless.

I'm sorry for him because he can't see she's only trying it on. Ought to have Emmies and Oscars and Oliviers. But there, he's always been a damn fool where she's concerned, though he knows nobody likes her, including himself.

Went over with him this Sat. and distinctly saw look of disappointment on her face when she realized he not alone. Well, I was only there because of doing my duty. I am her daughter-in-law, after all. I know what's what.

Upstairs in bed with daily nurse. Red and black pills size small cigars. Strange to see that vast bulk all crammed into one poor little bed.

And stranger still to think someone once fancied her like that.

Asked me to wash her teeth. S. down below, heating soup. Didn't refuse, but took them away and did it with eyes shut. Afterwards threw up down bathroom basin.

Wish I loved her. It would make it all so much easier.

Letter come for S. saying old job available due falling numbers in West Germany. Fail see how W. Germany affects S.E. London, but he right over moon. Should have made *Six O'Clock News*.

Dora said *On the house* when she heard, though she winced a bit when she saw how many people we'd got with us.

'Mrs Spink,' my daughter says to me in lull, holding an empty glass at me for microphone. 'So he's got his job back, you've just lost yours. Tell us what your emotions are, this moment in time.'

'Could have happened if we'd both been boys,' I said into the glass. Let her chew on that.

'Then you wouldn't have been married,' she says, lowering the glass.

Little smarty arsey.

We come away well after closing time and I had 'eadache the next morning.

But Stanley's whammy pains completely gone.

Balls to Mr Bangelstein all over house.

Caught me bending over bed just as I was slipping pig and hottie between covers.

I said, 'Oh, you great brute!'

And he said just 'That's right,' and sort of went ahead and when I twisted round to look he had big, big smile on his face like bloody Sunspan orange.

House like new pin. Mahogany toilet seat arrived. He fixed it and I washed in bleach. Gold plated bits to come.

Garden had a tidy up and all. Put that bloody, baggy uniform in incinerator. Smouldering nicely when thought she might come asking for it. Pulled it out all black and charred and smoking. Amy's belt suffered too.

Saved belt and stuffed uniform back in fire.

Sod her.

Death of a Countess

I can't believe it.

She's gone.

That great mountain of lard will never waddle into my front room again.

Went with him to see her in the mortuary where she's been laid out, massive great bundle on a slab, wrapped up in a black cloth, just the face showing and that with a silly little gauze veil laid over it.

Hiding the peppery brown whiskers.

I never seen anything so strange. She was all waxy. No wonder they call us the White race.

So still – yet she might move any minute.

God forbid.

He didn't say anything. Just took the veil away and

threw it crossly on the floor. Then he bent down and kissed her.

I was sad.

Then he went out without waiting for me and I was left alone with her. Still worried she might move, but saddened further still by those brown whiskers. She looked so defenceless somehow. Took nail scissors out of handbag and snipped them close and blew the ends away. Then I picked up the veil and put it decently back.

The little nurse that found her came in, the one that fetched him the night she had to go to hospital. She was very nice and quiet, just stood sort of respectfully at the back. Later gave us an envelope of Countess' small belongings like her watch, also her teeth, and the little suitcase I'd packed for her to take in, with things just as I'd packed them. Signed a little chitty to say we'd got all, she very kind and helpful and sympathetic.

Shall add her name to obituary notice in local paper – 'With special thanks to . . .' So nice and fitting.

Went to see undertaker and choose a coffin. He dived in first one he could find, with me tugging his elbow saying Gooch and Ducket down Lee High Road cheapo, not to mention Co-op.

Didn't listen. Picked a middle range after saying 'Anything.' Pointed out to him that top range were a rip off. It's all going to be underground anyway. Still, didn't want cheapo for fear of looking mean.

Funeral parlour very nice and tasteful, piped organ music, wax flowers everywhere and floral tributes arriving every five minutes for the dear departed, but not home.

Got back to *Semper Idem* and made huge pot of tea. Put brandy in his.

No nooky.

* * *

132

Went over to her place and through all her poor little effects.

While there, girl from Council rang to say rent in arrears. I said, 'Do you mind? There's been a death here.'

Could hear her giggling and laughing, chatting with other girls in office. She said, 'Can you speak up. A lot of background noise.'

I said, 'A death. There's been a death. Get that? There won't be no rent paid, 'cause none's due. All right, Clothears?' And I slammed down the phone. Well, he wasn't in a fit state to deal with things like that.

He in tears once, going through some photos in a drawer she'd kept.

Nothing much in her Post Office book, and of course her pension stops right there with her.

£200 in her current account with Nat. West.

£1,000 in Granny Bonds.

Three fivers paper-clipped together, loose pound coins (7), three fifties, a twenty, two tens and a jar full of little baby halfpence that went out of tender years ago.

And that was the Countess' estate. Pitiful, for one so huge in body. Didn't even have Access Card, none of your drastic plastic stuff at all.

Things weren't too tidy, but then she's never been what you might call a really clean person.

He said, 'What do you expect? She's bin ill.'

Well, I know, I know. But some of that dirt's been in corner of the kitchen floor for ages. Didn't say anything. Expect her great bulk stopped her getting down and anyway she's not here to defend herself, a bit like having whiskers when you're lying dead on mortuary slab for all to see.

When he wasn't looking, gouged out kitchen corners with her potato peeler. He found it on draining board later and said, 'We'll take this, shall we? It's always been a good'un.'

Then I got on with her clothes upstairs in wardrobe

133

while he was sorting garden stuff. Later bundled it all into black plastic sacks. Was in mind to take it down the Sue Ryder, but who would buy it? Only a camping shop. Put sacks out with all the other rubbish and left 50p on top for dustmen. He didn't want to know.

Over there again today (Mon.). Got to hurry. Council want keys Wednesday, anyway his half days end this week. Rent girl rang again. Told her to get stuffed with rough end of pineapple.

I said inhuman to him, this wanting out by Wednesday, but he just shrugged and said life.

Just her furniture to go now. She never had many books or pictures, just mirrors, which I gave Dorelia, and TV set, hired.

Nobody wanted furniture. Rang all round, even Salvation Army. Called a junk man in in the end and got fifty quid the lot. He said, 'No call for this ugly old Art Deco style these days.'

S. sad to see sideboard hoisted in to lorry.

Funeral three days' time, Friday, 28 February, twelve o'clock, Crystal Palace District.

Found out from Wayne could have got much better price for furniture from thrusting London dealer. Didn't mench to Stan.

Notice published In Memoriam column local rag, well, Deaths. Had wanted to have one of those rhyming tributes, it shows feeling and indeed, had just happened to compose one.

Gone before, dear Mum, you were so brave.
Hope to see you the other side of the grave.
Remembered always, January and June.
Much loved and missed, like a never-forgotten tune.

But Stanley wasn't having any.

People at house by eleven. Flo and Vi in marroon and dark mauve, quite tasteful. D. in nave, very nice, also Amy. Eamonn, thank God, still weak.

Wore my pinstripe with feature pearlized buttons and a little black hat with feathers at the back and eye-level veil. Saw Flo look as if thinking *Over the top.*

Let her.

Some lovely, tasteful floral tributes from neighbours and ex-employer, showing sensitivity and careing.

At 11.45 Countess arrived in the middle range coffin. I wanted to put all the floral tributes on top of her with the tickets showing. People like to see what they've sent, and others too. Man in black rearranged them all.

Annoyed.

Earth in Cemetry banked up prettily under bright green plastic grass; thought very good idea and toyed with getting some for *Semper Idem* (front) but don't think he would wear it.

He very quiet and still, even when they threw token handful of earth in on to lowered coffin. They do it with ropes.

He stayed looking down into hole when service over. Roderick touched him gently on the arm and he started.

Annoyed. I should have been the one to do that.

Had made ham sandwiches and large trifle, also jelly, nuts, cheeses and little biscuits with pate on them. Linen tablecloth and red paper serviettes. Funny to think last time I had that cloth out she was here too.

Vi into sherry. Dorelia held up well. People stuffing trifle.

'I'll be next, you see,' Vi telling everyone.

So she will if she goes on like that.

Stan in a corner, Wayne going round with sherry. All

eyeing each other after a bit thinking someone ought to say a few words but not me, when door bell went and I jumped, thinking My God, Eamonn.

But very tall, distinguished gentleman. Hat off as soon as he saw me. About seventy, but very upright. Oo-er. If he'd been a touch younger, wouldn't have said no, if he'd asked me nicely.

'Mrs Spink?' he asked, sounding like The Queen, not feminine, I don't mean, but very upper class. (Well, she is; you can't really go any higher, can you?) 'I hesitate to intrude at this time, but wondered if I might be permitted to attend the ceremony?'

Not many people talk to you like that.

'My name is Devereux,' he said, holding out a card. 'Edward Devereux.'

I took his little card but hardly looked.

'You're too late,' I told him. 'It's all over. We buried her this morning.'

He seemed cut up by this, not that he showed it much, it was more the look in his eyes.

'You come on in,' I said. 'We can give you a sherry. My son-in-law will do the honours.'

'Oh, thank you,' he says. 'If you're positive I don't intrude?'

I held the door open wide and he come in and immediately took off his hat (which he'd put back on again) a thing I've nagged Stanley six, silly and sideways about for thirty years. He will wear a flat 'at in the house, right into the bedroom, if I don't go at him. Forgets he's got it on.

Took Edward Devereux in and introduced him round. Didn't seem shy, just held his hand out to everyone like a superstar greeting fans. Even nodded pleasantly to one or two of the Countess' neighbours who'd come back, I didn't bother with. Was a bit ashamed of Vi, though. She sort curtseyed, bobbed about in front of him. No behaviour for a Purkiss.

136

He was a long time shaking hands with Stanley.

I looked meaningfully at those neighbours and they scarpered, things to do, places they gotta go.

Then in two minds what to do about the aunts.

He was over by the french windows with Stan, looking out and admiring my little blue pond.

'Much of a garden yourself, have you?' I asked him.

'Quite large,' he said. 'Though most of it's given over to Highland cattle and so forth.'

'You got cattle, you must have a park,' I told him, not entirely joking and he smiled (dead attractive in spite of his age) and said yes, he had.

'You a farmer?'

'No, no. Though we have the Home Farm nearby on the Estate of course.'

Oh, of course. And then it come to me.

He had a Stately Home.

'You have another little drink,' I told him. 'My son-in-law will oblige.'

Aunt Vi was doing something ludicrous with peanuts. You could see her plate. I made Florrie take her out while I made Edward Devereux a nice little collation on a red serviette.

'My connection with Mrs Spink, your mother,' he was saying as I moved towards him, 'goes back a long way. We knew each other many years ago.' His eyes were clouding over again. 'She worked – *had a domestic situation* – in Norfolk, as no doubt, you know.'

'She was in service. She was 'ousemaid at Burlingham Hall,' Stan said.

'Yes. And in those far off days, I was the younger son of the house.'

Well. I could guess what was coming. All that reading of Aurora North-Brightley had prepared me, hadn't it.

'You're *Lord* Burlingham,' I said.

He waved a depredating hand. 'No, no. My elder brother. But you don't want to hear about all that.'

137

He could have stepped straight out of the pages of a North-Brightley novel. Aurora would have *loved* him.

'The long and short of it is,' he said, gazing at Stan with engaging, though manly frankness, 'I loved your mother once, and she loved me. Before she met and married – er – your father, of course. Our love was, as they say, doomed from the start.'

Well, Aurora, old darling, put that in your typewriter and suck on it.

'The War came,' he went on. 'I was sent abroad. The War changed everything. She had married, I heard later. And she had a child.'

'Yes,' our Stan said proudly. 'Me.'

'Ah,' this Edward Devereux said and looked at Stanley a long, long time.

He recovered himself though, accepted another sherry and then asked our permission to go and lay flowers on her grave. We all went to the door to see him out – not that there was much danger of *him* pinching the spoons – and he waltzled off, not replacing the hat till he got to the gate.

Looked back and waved just once – at Stan. I stood in the hall behind him feeling gobsmacked.

'Most probably a con man,' Roderick remarked behind *me*.

'What?' I said, spinning round.

'A confidence trickster. Come to see what valuables you've got in the house. What better time when everyone's thoughts are on something else? I saw him looking round.'

'You're barmy,' I told him.

Amy helped me clear plates and glasses. Vi was let back into the room, demanding to know what she'd missed. But I was wondering how Edward Devereux would feel if he'd known the young woman he'd loved had died a huge barrel of a body crammed into a cheap(ish) pine coffin, and, but for me and my little scissors, whiskers like downy moths fluttering round her face.

No one said anything to Stan. Later I found him doing little sums with an old calculator D. left behind, and checking them with pencil and paper. (Our generation didn't use no calculators.) Sums looked like years added up to me. But I didn't say anything neither.

I washed up. Then I went back into the lounge where he was sitting in the dark.

'Want the light on?'

'If you like.'

'Maybe that's where I get my feeling for the country from.'

'Maybe.'

'Runs deep in the bone, you know, that kind of thing. Blood will out.'

'Yeah.'

Silence.

''Course, if true, this will mean she's half noble.'

'Who?'

'Dorelia.'

I thought about it.

'Quarter,' I corrected him. 'If true.'

'Yeah,' he said. 'If true.'

We sat on for some time.

'I'll make the Ovaltine,' he said at last. 'Makes you think.'

'Ovaltine?'

'That your ancestors came over with the Conqueror.'

'Don't you put sugar in,' I said. 'Use that Nutrasweet. And don't give yourself airs. My lot were already here.'

'Yeah, getting up everybody's nose,' he said.

We laughed.

'You in a good mood, then, 'Reen?' he asked.

Plum losing interest in her children. Yesterday one tried to feed so she smacks him round the ear. And when she's not there they try to mount each other.

Wayne has christened them Tit and Tot.
R. says for Chrissake have them done.

Days long and grey. Not fear of falling off world any more, rather feeling of sitting at bottom of deep, deep, deep, dark well. Everything passing me by, overhead.
D. says lack Vitamin B Complex.

Got bot. B Complex from 'Nutmeg'.
Still down well.
D. saying everything down to nutrition in the end.
But *everything*?
'What about your father with his chips and beer?' I asked her. 'Nothing ever wrong with him, just makes him sexy.'
She said, 'Count your blessings, Mum.'
Cheeky little baby.

Out to Peckham secretly to 'Nutmeg'. Bought large size yoghurt and pollyunsaturated oil. Also some carob-coated chocolate biscuits because they looked so nice in the picture on the front.
If he gives up chips and beer will it make him feel less sexy?

Well, no. Said oil made chips all soggy, also biscuits tasted like they'd been eaten once already.
Also, 'How much that yoghurt cost?' And when I told him – 'Blimey, saw you coming, didn't they?'

Putting it back on again. Ten bloody stone. D. says got to want to stop eating. Tell yourself. Do it when you're relaxed. Speak direct to your subconscious mind.
Knitted three little matinee jackets and five woolly pairs bootees, sort she had when young in yellow because thought perhaps after all you can't really trust that scan machine.

140

She said thankyou and put them away in a drawer. Had a good look. Nothing in there that you'd call pretty at all, just a lot of little bags with strings.

Told her, 'It's a good idea to have wool next to his skin, you know.'

She said, 'Her skin, Mummy and don't worry you've got to knit a lot of things, they do marvellous little clothes in Marks.'

Annoyed.

Just hope little Baby likes her tomato-type Gro-bags, that's all. Treating her like plant in a greenhouse, is what *I* think.

Monday, 5 March

My dear Sister round with big bunch primroses she'd picked down Petts Wood woods. (Nat. Truss.)

'Lovely there,' she says, all wistful. 'Ever such nice houses.'

'You'd be homesick,' I told her sharply. Could just see what was coming. She's a soppy thing, but she's the only one I got.

'Gimme here,' I said. 'We got shops and red buses. And you can get to Victoria in thirteen minutes.'

'And there's a lovely pub,' she went on. 'The Daylight Inn, all timbered up, does jumbo sausage in french bread.'

'Just another gin palace,' I said and made her some tea and gave her the rest of the carob biscuits to finish up.

Her primroses and catkins sat in my blue vase on the kitchen windowsill in a patch of sun.

Her and her Petts Wood.

Still . . .

When we lived in Spitalfields, one room at Mum's, in the 'Fifties, all Pakkies now and clothing retailers, I had this dream, long before he started to do well in furniture. George Harrison and *Hard Day's Night* indeliably

141

associated with applying for our first mortgage, something Mum had never heard of. We was Yuppies then before the name was thought of.

I was looking for semidetached because it doesn't seem natural somehow to live on your own without neighbours you can't hear. And it was way before amplifiers and ghettoblasters and so on, so noise like that didn't bother me like it do now. No. And what I mostly wanted anyway was a little curved cement path in front and a clipped hedge and flower beds all neat with African marigolds in rows for summer because the petals don't come off. Also net curtains, fitted carpets and a modern kitchen.

'Don't want much, do you?' Mum said at the time.

Shame she had to go and die before she see I got it all at last.

Now this Petts Wood . . .

You got to have something to aim at. I read that in Claire Rayner.

Tried the delicate approach with him.

'How you feel about living in Petts Wood?'

'About as 'appy as elephant up a tree.'

'No, no! Gimme definite answer!' I cried.

'Good place to train spot,' he admitted grudgingly. 'But otherwise I think the idea's barmy.'

Well of course, Purkisses don't give up easy.

'Is it so wrong to want everything all nice?' I asked him, wistful like our Amy.

'Blimey, Mog, you got everything nice,' he said. 'Is it that I haven't cut the blimming hedge?'

'I just had this dream, that's all,' I said, like Martin Luther King. 'Quiet, respectable road, no lager cans, with trees. Trees growing outa pavements, that's genteel. Pillarbox on the corner maybe, but no filling stations, no allotments with tatty little 'uts, bus garages, anything industrial and scrubby. Residential. Wouldn't have to take a holiday from there.'

142

'Oh, it's the *holiday*,' he said. 'But you said not to this year, not with the baby coming . . .'

Flounced out to the kitchen all huffy to make toast. Well, no Mars Bars in the house.

'Should have thought Petts Wood more fitting for your bloody noble blood!' I shouted back.

Constant dripping weareth away a stone.

That's in the Bible somewhere and I must say it was a surprise when someone told me. Fancy the Bible knowing how to deal with men.

Describes my methods exactly.

He eyed my piled-up plate when I come back.

'Some for you,' I said, divvying up and fetching his tea in one of the rude mugs Wayne bought.

He sat and munched his toast and butter and honey and we watched *News at Ten* and then we went up to bed and I was in a good, good, *good* mood.

He was still panting a little with his eyes shut and drifting away sweetly when I spoke again.

'Wouldn't half like to live in Petts Wood,' I told him.

Spoke direct to his subconscious mind.

Back on diet. Found suspender belt and fixed it. S. very, very happy when he saw the bra.

Sewed three pink Gro-bags for our baby girl.

'Look at it, 'Reen,' he says to me last night. 'Feel it. Measure it for size.'

Again? Maybe he's worried that they shrink with age.

'I read in Dr David Delvin they're all the same when up.'

'Poo – *doctors*,' he said. 'All the same.'

'What I said.' But I fetched a tape measure just to keep the peace.

Sixteen centimetres.

'Speak to me in Imperial!' he implored. 'Bloody foreign don't mean a thing. That's no way to measure a man's virility, in twaddling little bits.'

143

I had a certain sympathy. I won't use Metric either generally, nor the Post Code nor any other bloody silly little Gumment numbers, trying to cut things up and reduce us all the time.

'Want to know how seven and 'alf Imperial inches feels?' he asked.

Oh God, I've known for thirty years. But I let him show me, his hands flexing and reflexing in delight over the peephole, tit-filled bra.

'Like a rock, eh?' he said, going to work with thrusting vigour.

I let him get on with it. Hopeless to try and join him. Days when I used to come, *crying*, because it was so bloody lovely, are all over.

Afterwards he said in this hurt, small voice, 'Was it all right?' – as if he'd seen how sad I was, and knew.

I was surprised. I said, 'No, never is these days, somehow,' and then we were both surprised at me being honest.

He said, after a bit, 'You never said. All this time? How long? I thought you always come.'

And I said, 'No. Not any more. Not for some time.'

Well he lay there, thinking, and then without saying anything he used his middle finger the way he used to do when we were courting and I came. It was all right.

Maybe should write to Dr David Delvin about this. But have mislaid the pullout, regional, anonymity-guaranteed sex survey questionnaire he published in his magazine *She* this month.

Perhaps he'd appreciate a private letter.

'How much is Dad grieving over Granny?' Dorelia asked me on the phone tonight and I replied guardedly, 'The usual, so far as I know.'

Well he looks back to when he was a little boy sometimes, wistful, like Amy and me with Petts Wood. But the mother who was there then was not the mountain with the whiskers who just died.

144

I said, 'How you?' and D. said fine, little Jane jumping. Going to be Prime Minister by the feel of things.

'Surely you want something more feminine for her than that?' I said.

And she said sharply, 'She'll do anything she wants. There'll be no gender stereotyping for this little child.'

And I thought back to this friend of mine, Josy, at school, and how she desperately wanted to be an engineer and couldn't, in the 'Fifties. Poor Josy. Wonder what she did.

Crocuses out in lines in beds in front. Sunny.

Gave Tit and Tot to friend of Amy's at the URC, a good home, if religious.

Glad they've gone. Apart from endless bonking, in habit of digging up little dead brother from his place under lilac tree and rolling him about.

Given up on news of small blind sister.

D. rang again this morning, great excitement. Matron Peebles featuring in local rag.

Great, thought I. They've jumped on her for fraud; missappreciation of the old dears' funds.

Already sunny mood got turbo boost.

'No, no,' D. said. 'A fire. Been a heroine. But I'm not telling you. Go get your bloody own.'

Rushed out and bought copy of paper.

Front page news, with photographs.

Firemen at the scene last night confirmed the fire originated on the second floor.

'Things might have been much worse,' a spokesperson for the Fire Service said. 'But for the responsible, swift action of the Chief Nursing Officer, many more lives would have undoubtedly been lost.'

The dead woman is named as Miss Irene Cropper, MBE, aged 78, and ex(Wartime) Wren Officer and long-term resident of Belvedere Grange.

145

Felt like ringing in to ask if Delft and Davenport all right, but didn't.

Plum run over by a car.

Didn't stop. I ran out in slippers into main road, screaming.

Scooped her up. Still warm. Guts crushed and oozing out backside. Looked up at me as if about to speak.

Put her on the settee. Think she went then, soon as I laid her down.

Phoned Amy, who came round at once with Glenlivet and a box of Kleenex.

Cried.

'If I could get the bastard,' I told her, 'I'd have torn his balls off by now – no, that's not right, I'd have left them hanging by a thread so he'd keep thinking there was hope, then I'd have pulled them off and tied them to a string and kep' it dangling over his face so he couldn't help but see.'

Amy sighed. 'That driver might not even have seen Plum there. Cats streak about.'

I said, 'Don't gimme that. Just pour the Scotch.'

Had a tankard.

'Why, Amy, why?' I asked her and she shook her head. She don't know any more than the poor little fella with the watery eyes on the front doorstep.

All I know is, *I* didn't make the bloody world.

If I had I'd have done it a bit better.

Amy believes God done it in six days, then had to send His only son to make it right again.

Look what they did to him.

What sort of loving Father would do that?

'This is a shitty place,' I told her.

'And we got more than most to be thankful for,' she said.

Sometimes I can't see it.

146

But after a bit I calmed down. Wrapped Plum up in a clean tea towel and buried her next to her baby under the tree.

Haven't done any housework today.

He said, 'We'll get another one.'

I said, 'No, I want Plum.'

Went upstairs and had another howl.

No more cats.

Or dogs, or anything you give your bloody heart to.

Ever.

Sewed six pink Gro-bags and watched yukky soaps.

Ain't they got any real red blood, the Aussies and the Yanks?

The poor provincials.

Ate five Mars Bars.

Uncle Dick.

D. pleased with bags, prattled happily. Didn't tell her about Plum.

'Any day now,' she said. 'My calculations are way ahead of the hospital's.'

'Oh? You never told me,' I said.

And she said shyly (for her), 'Well, you know when you've made love, don't you?'

Sure as hell do. Still exhausted from going five rounds with her father, though naturally didn't tell her that.

The young don't like to think their parents do it.

Deep, deep, deep down inside well.

What's it all about?

All those bloody years, then out like a bloody light.

Burned Plum's basket in incinerator. Took her bowls down the Sue Ryder where woman washed them and put in front of window.

Bought them back for 50p.

* * *

147

Sitting down in well this morning doing 0. Apparently there's a limit to number of Gro-bags even little Baby Girl requires.

Phone rang.

Nothing. Thought wrong number.

Rang again in afternoon. This time young voice, wanting her *Pink Panther*. Woman.

Said, 'Wrong number, dear,' and hung up quickly.

And stood thinking.

He busy up in loft this evening. Took him a cup of tea and while on ladder said, 'The phone went twice today.'

'So?' he said, busy.

'Who'd you think it could have been?'

'I don't know, do I?' he said testily.

'Keep your hair on,' I told him, going down.

Cruel thing to say to Stan.

Stuffed lambs' hearts.

Streaky rashers.

Peas and grilled tomatoes.

Roast potatoes.

Savoury gravy.

Pond pudding, lemon sauce.

Homemade dairy ice cream.

Or liver and onions, maybe. Such a pig for that and oniony for hours on end.

Or con carne, loadsagarlic.

Thing that puts you off the Pink Panther's loving is his stinky breath.

Or am I being fanciful again? Because where does he find the time?

Young man in 'SteamPast'.

'Yes, madam – can I help you?'

148

'Hope so,' I told him. 'Looking for Sharon . . . I forget her other name.'

Stared at me and went reluctantly to ask in back.

'She left,' he said, coming out again.

'Any idea where she went?'

'No.'

So helpful. I charged out.

Stopped off at new Tesco's. Place gets more like a cathedral every day. Feeling shaky.

Liver.

And now what?

Waiting, waiting. First lot of courage gone.

No longer down well, out on huge dry plain now, under a burning sky. Wind hot and scary. Where do these images keep coming from?

When he come in I said, 'Had a good day?' and he said, 'Not particularly. What's for tea?'

Had it on trays watching *Six O'Clock News*. Afterwards he said, 'Very tasty.'

Tried to hold back and be subtle and everything but it come out different as usual.

Said, 'You having an affair?'

He jumped. 'Why you saying that?'

'Oh, one thing and another. Wanna watch the magazine programme or would you rather I switched over to *The Pink Panther Show*?'

'You what?'

'You heard. Well?'

'Well what?'

'Are you?'

'Am I what?'

'Having an affair?'

'Barmy,' he said, folding the *Daily Mail* in halves and then in quarters. 'You know that?'

'Well?'

149

Didn't answer.

I went up to bed. Kept pig and hottie over my side. Couldn't sleep. Felt him come up, get in and lie on far side of the bed, millions of miles away across the dry and burning plain. Lay like that all night.

Pretended to be still asleep when he got up this morning.

''Reen!' he hissed but I thought, Bugger you, and lay still with my eyes tight shut.

After a bit I heard the front door shut.

Went up Job Centre and got job at Piggi's Pizza, to start Mon. Might as well.

Went round Amy's but she out, Church coffee morning or some such rubbish. Typical.

Went down Dorelia's but she out too, probably antenatal.

Went up High Street and bought three summer frocks in BhS.

Met the Larches at the gate coming home. Smiled to show I was broadminded and felt face stiff from not smiling for so long. Then thought saw Eamonn weaving about back in main road so rushed in and shut door. Larches surprised.

It wasn't Eamonn.

He come in with a face I didn't know. He was a stranger. Knew he'd been with her. Distant. Had her look.

Didn't speak and I said, 'We got to sort this out.'

He said wearily, 'We bin through all this before. Nothing to sort out.'

'Oh no? You're carrying on and there's nothing to sort out?'

He said, 'I'm not carrying on. Whatever there was, if anything, was all in your mind and I thought over, weeks ago. She got my train bits, that's all. Well, she flirted, but that's nothing. She flirts with all the blokes.'

'What she see in you?' I felt savage. 'You're old and fat and you haven't any hair.'

150

'Thanks a lot,' he said. 'You really know how to make a bloke feel like a king.'

'Well, but what?' I persisted.

'I dunno,' he said pettishly. 'Perhaps she likes father figures.'

'You already got a daughter,' I reminded him.

Another night lying either end of the dry plain.

A day down Il Piggi's is crash course in how to serve up Salmonella most attractively. All too busy running restaurant to care much about customers.

Big Mick, tall, sweaty man with slicked-back hair, says managers of pizza parlours last a year on average. Last one retired with ulcers, twenty-four. So far Mick's been here fifteen months. Gets in at six. Don't leave for home until eleven. Six days a week. Sunday, the VAT.

I said, 'What's left is your free time?'

He didn't laugh.

I sweep floors and wash them, wipe tables, clear crockery and wash up in kitchen. Brought gloves and plastic apron after that first day.

Thunderous heavy metal rock most of the time. Job-dodgers in the morning, old ladies in the afternoon. Golden oldies for the old girls; Andy Williams, Frank Sinatra.

(Dorelia said 'Frank who?')

No one allowed to have just coffee. Must order eats as well. Pizzas speciality, even tastier dropped on the floor face down so grit gets in the cheese. Said something and Mick snapped wouldn't happen if floors swabbed properly.

Don't think I shall last here long.

Mind, as much Black Forest Gato as can eat allowed, also redcurrant cheesecake, lemon sponge and something called pineapple frosties. Great freezers out back stacked full of the stuff. Corrugated iron roof. Dismal place.

Washing up machine old and funny. Works, though. Load up on round tray on circular wheel, then push back in and close lid. Huge scalding jets, then plates steaming-gleaming quite a treat.

Ghost-person works at night, doing late shift. Sometimes leaves little notes: *To Person Responsible For Mornings* . . .

Cheek.

Always leave everywhere neat and nice but she likes things her way.

Get in at eight quite easily. Can walk, as only in Whitehorse Lane.

Started sweeping between tables in front part today, chairs up and stacked, music already loud. Jackie and Trace, who wait at tables, lolling about pinning on Piggi bibs and smoking, rubbish passers-by outside in the street.

Trace said, 'Look at that fat geezer with that little baby tart.'

Spun round and looked but of course it wasn't. Trace said, 'Can't stand cradle snatchers. Toy boys is one thing but old men are dirty.'

Just what I think.

Bomb. Sharon (ex-train shop) now at DemiPlan, in checkout DIY and Homecare Dept., back of warehouse and unloading bay. Told me so hisself.

Friday. My day off in lieu. Went down to Lewisham to see what I could see.

Old alley full of tat, blown paper, empty lager cans. Whistling March wind and me crouching by DemiPlan's factory wall, holding coat round me, feeling foolish.

Ashamed, too, of me and of him. With home so neat and pretty just up the way and this so dirty and somehow ugly. *Sordid.* Shuddered at thought of Dorelia or Amy knowing what I was doing. Pride.

Snuck out past derelict yard with SOLD notice on board leaning in breeze out into road. Don't know what I'd thought I'd see, only aware of depression.

Thought I might find a Wimpy or a MacDonald's then and get some tea or coffee.

Something called 'Kay's Pantry', pseudo-posh, but it looked clean. Check tablecloths, waitress in black frock. Thought that went out with dinosaurs.

Ordered pot of tea for one. Up close, the place was shitty, fly dirts on walls and cigarette ash in (white) sugar basin, brown sauce stains on cloth. Thought I'd go home.

Then in she came.

Had two mates with her. Frizzy, straw-coloured hair and long, thin legs gave me instant shock of recognition, also high, nasal voice.

Felt bad and unhappy, horribly excited and almost sick. Looked away out of the window at the paper scraps whirling in dusty spirals and wondered if she'd seen and recognized me. Noway could I escape. She was between me and the door.

They sat down and ordered and she talked, I forget what about except she moaned they expected miracles of her, down at the DemiPlan checkout. The whiny little voice imprinted itself on my brain. Unforgettably. Think I shall be able to hear it till the day that I die.

They had a junk food lunch, iced buns and orangeade, then they got up to go and oh yes, she'd seen me. Didn't look over, but there was *large* smirk on her face, unmistakable. They swanned off and I was left. No one else came in. Not surprised.

Paid bill and got up to go feeling heavy. Walked outside and stood on pavement and thought how all the twists and turns of my life had lead only to . . . this cold moment on a gusty road in a dirty London suburb, alone.

Went home.

*   *   *

Not talking much. He come in usual time. I get shopping on way home, four-thirty.

Reading back in diary: 'Life just isn't worth living now my little girl has gone . . .'

Sentimental twaddle. Now I'd give anything to be back there, last November.

No wouldn't. All this would be still to come.

Fished out second Valentine, one with UNKNOWN ADMIRER in big letters. Put it ostensibly on mantel-piece.

He said quietly, 'I sent that.'

Threw it in bin. (Me.)

He said nothing.

Rows. And when we're not rowing, not talking. Only five days and one weekend, but quite enough.

Work very hard on feet but glad to get out of house. Usually leave breakfast dishes and bed unmade. At work, feel as if treading on thorns, feet so hot. Reduced to wearing nasty black shoes from Grange days.

Thorns in head, too.

Glad to leave, get back home. Then he comes in and there's a chronic silence.

He said, 'Can't stand much more of this. Why don't you see a doctor?'

'I don't need no doctor,' I told him.

'But you do, Moggy, you do.'

And so it goes on. And not a bit of How's your father.

Found Plum's old rubber mouse and took it up Cator Park Sports Ground and threw it away as far as it would go.

Didn't ask me where I been when I got in. Not even a clumsy cuddle when he saw me crying.

Moved all his things into spare room. Put D.'s things up in loft, beside his trains.

154

He blinked a bit, but said nothing. Just looked at me sadly until I wanted to scream.

Feeble little attempt at joke: 'Wasser matter, you want all the bed now?'

'Yes, I do. You can lie in there, dreaming about your tart.'

'I've told you and told you and told you. There's nothing in it. *Nothing*. What do you have to keep making such a blasted fool of yourself for?'

'Well, you would say that,' I pointed out.

'But it's true!'

'Also true that whore got job down DemiPlan,' I told him. 'Who got her there, you or some other bloke the floosie fancies?'

He sighed heavily and turned away, guilt written all over him.

The beat goes on. Big Mick asked if I wanted to quit dishwashing and wait on tables but one look at my face made him add, 'Well no, perhaps not.'

Any other time I would have jumped at the offer. The Piggi bibs aren't unattractive and that way you swan around. As it is, prefer to stay out of sight. Me and my gloomy, frozen face are better in the kitchen.

Getting very, very hot occasionally these days. Starts as a tingly feeling, the way when you were sick as a little kid, then horrid feeling something nasty going to happen, then full flush so you put your red face where no one's going to see. Told Amy about it when I was having one. She said, 'Is that it? I never noticed.'

Gone right off cheesecake. First week I scoffed as much as I could hold, cramming it in with both hands. Now attraction worn off and wonder why.

Still cooking for him, washing socks and shirts and pants (machine) and doing chores, but 'Reen Spink has slipped out somewhere and gone missing. Spirit of *Semper Idem*

155

simply isn't there. Empty shell zooming around like zombie. I dropped poor 'Reeny somewhere and can't pick her up again. Lying in a ditch somewhere, perhaps.

Very formal evenings this week. After tea goes straight up to his trains, Saturday down the pub. I stayed home. Suppose that's when he saw her.

Lay awake Sat. night, couldn't sleep, heard him come in. Later padded out for pee (me) and the house seemed different, full of alien things. Can't stand this. Think I'm going round the twist. Shall end up undeliably out to lunch.

He came in late for dinner Sunday morning. Roast all tepid. Was uninclined to row, too tired.

Said, 'Sorry, Mog, I . . .'

'Don't you call me Mog!' I told him. Shouted loud.

Dunno what Larches thought, that coming through the wall. We don't shout as a rule.

''Ullo. Sweetness and light as usual,' he said sarcastic. 'What've I done now?'

Nearly hit him.

'Done?' I said. 'You know the full extent of that.'

'What you mean?'

'You know what I mean.'

'No I don't, honest.'

'Honest is what you ain't.'

'M—'Reen!' he said. 'Please listen. Please.'

'I will not.'

'Please!'

'Get out!' I shrieked. 'Go and find your hussy. Shack up with her, just don't waste any more of my time. God knows I've given you enough all ready. Go on, get out!'

'You don't mean that.'

'I do. I do mean it. Thirty bloody years and all . . .'

He held up a hand. 'Don't go on.'

'I will go on!'

156

'Hush,' he said. 'Here's Roderick and Amy.'

But it wasn't. It was those bloody, old-maid nosey parkers from next door.

He left me standing there by the cooker (I was trembling) and went and opened the back door.

'Glorious news!' said two breathy little-girl voices. 'You know dear Mr Thomson from the corner of Khartoum Crescent? We know him at church, of course, – that's St Francis' – where he's a sidesman, and we caught him up outside Woolworth's this morning and what *do* you think he had to tell us?'

'*Spit it out!*' I (very nearly) shrieked.

'Well, that there's a little cat living apparently wild under his tool shed on his allotment patch.'

'Not just now, sorry,' Stanley said. 'Another time perhaps.'

'Oh, but we remembered how you'd lost your . . .'

'Thanks. Very kind of you,' Stanley said.

'We thought we must just tell you in case . . .'

They began to back away, still twittering, and he closed the door on them. Another time I'd have told him off for rudeness, but not now. He come back brooding.

'Bound to come round, they hear a row like that,' he grumbled. 'You lower your voice, 'Reen. Probably thought I was hammering you.'

I'd give anything sometimes if he'd only rough me up a bit.

Shows they care, dunnit?

Someone said that once, somewhere else in another world.

'Dinner's ready,' I told him.

He had the telly on while we ate, farming and weather reports. Covered the need for conversation.

Rice pudding.

'No thanks,' he said and got up to cut himself some cheese.

'You being purposely offensive?'

157

Sighed heavily. 'Thought you was, rice pudd'n' on a Sunday.'

I sighed heavily.

He went up to muck about with trains.

Mick asked again if I would like to waitress.

'You don't look your age, you know,' he said.

Thanks.

Muttered at him about being too big and he said, 'No, straight up. You could lose a few pounds, maybe, not a lot. And *smile*. You're good-looking but it's no good showing the customers face like a week of Sundays.'

Soon as I could, snuck off to Ladies and examined face. He's right. Advantage of having round one is fat plumps the wrinkles out.

And have lost weight – about seven pounds.

Bought new lipstick in lunch hour, *Passionate Cerise*, and practised smiling in shop windows, frightening people. Face still stiff.

Sausages and mash and onions and baked beans with strong mustard sauce.

Marmalade pudding with lots of own jelly, custard and ice cream.

'This more like it,' he said. 'We friends again, then, Moggy?'

'Naturally not if you're still seeing your popsie.'

'Can't help see her, can I?'

'Can't *help*?'

'Well, she's there.'

'Oh?'

'Be reasonable?'

'Why, you little rat?'

Later he said, 'Going up the pub. You coming?'

Might as well.

No one in there that we knew, except by sight. Took our drinks to a little corner table where we could row

158

undisturbed. Dora looked at us, but she was busy.

'Look, Lo-g,' he began.

I sat up. 'Log?'

'I didn't say "Log", I said "Mog",' he said.

'You didn't. You said "Log".'

'Never.'

'Bloody liar.'

'Well, slip of the tongue, then.'

'*Slip of the tongue?*'

I did some very fast thinking very fast.

'I suppose she's got a nickname, this Sharon tart?'

'Maybe.'

'What?'

'Dunno.'

'You do. What is it?'

'Well, some of the blokes – and some of the girls – call her . . .'

'Yeah?'

'Lollipop.'

I see. No point in further arguing. He'd been about to call me by her name. I put down my drink. He stared.

'Where you going?'

'Home.'

'Home? But we've only had . . .'

I got up and went out and he stood up quickly to follow, then stopped and stood finishing his pint in hasty gulps. Then he followed me out, Dora watching us both keenly all the time.

Furious inside, very self-contained outside. Knew exactly what I had to do.

'Here, hold on, what you doing with that suitcase?' he asked, alarmed.

'Packing it.'

'Packing? You're not going? Hey, those are my socks.'

'Too right.'

Threw pants, socks, shirts and his weekend trousers into the open suitcase on the bed with wardrobe door open and me marching round bedroom searching for and finding things. He pattered after me like little lost dog.

'There!' I said and snapped that suitcase shut and handed it to him. He blinked.

'What'm I supposed to do with this?'

'Unpack it as you need the things.'

He blinked again. 'You throwing me out, 'Reen?'

'Right again.'

'But where'll I go? You can't mean this.'

'I don't care and I do mean it.'

'You don't.'

'I do.'

We stood for a long time in that bedroom where we slept. Then he took the case and turned away. Felt like snatching it back, cuddling him tight and saying didn't mean it, nasty mistake and all been dreadful dream. But then he spoke.

'I'll go to Amy's,' he said.

And he brightened.

Amy's.

'Are you so surprised?' he said, looking at me all steady.

'Yeah, well, you run to her, why don't you?' I said bitterly. 'Everyone does.'

He said nothing more. Even gave impression he was cheerful. Marched down the stairs, holding his little case and out into the night. Presently I heard the Metro start.

'You wimp!' I shouted after him for going.

House very, very still. Kept thinking he'd be back. Wandered out to kitchen and old smell of onions. Hour before in here I'd had a husband.

Found our tea plates with their mustard traces, marmalade pudding crumbs, all soggy with ice cream.

In sudden, awful paddy piled all four plates and dropped them. They shattered, mucky, blue Willow Pattern

160

pieces everywhere on floor. Stood staring at them horrified, then whimpering, fled upstairs, flung into bed and pulled covers up, right over head.

About two o'clock surfaced, got out, cleaned face and teeth, did hotties, set alarm.

On time for work this morning.

Life now very strange. Keep starting things to say to Stan, forgetting he not here. Bed huge and cold and silent without raspberry tarts. Don't bother cooking – at least kitchen stays neater that way.

Three days without a word from anyone. And constant, haunting thought: *whose side will Baby take?*

And always, hammer, hammer, hammer: you lose everything, 'Reeny, beginning with baby boy. Even the Willow Pattern four plates down.

Thinking should maybe set fire to house to complete picture, when Roderick at back door.

'Can I come in?' he asks, all polite for once.

I was sitting in semi-dark, not even telly on, remains of Birds Eye frozen meal for one beside me. Hastily cleared tray.

'Well?' I said. 'Stan sent you?'

'No.'

'What then?'

'Came because we're all concerned.'

'Oh yeah.'

'We love you.'

'We? Who's we?' I asked, even while mind grappling with new strong word. Not like our Roderick to use 'love'. Come to think of it, he didn't use it in the old days, even. Our family tend not to.

'Amy, me, Dorelia, Wayne, Fella – and Stan,' he said. 'You're being bloody silly.'

'So?'

'You're hurting Stan. He's done nothing.'

'Oh. Talked to you, has he?'

161

'Had to talk to somebody. No harm in that. Not disloyal.'

'Yes it is.'

'No. Anyway, all he said was you chucked him out.'

'And now he wants to come back, that it?'

'No. Though it would help us. He and Eamonn are having to share a room.'

'He doesn't want to come back even though he's sharing a room with *Eamonn*?'

'No.'

'*No?*'

'No. Not while you're all jealous and suspicious.'

'I got *reason* to be all jealous and suspicious.'

'Oh, I don't think so,' Roderick said easily.

'You don't know for sure.'

'No. No, I don't. But I know Stan. And I know your trouble. Pushing people away. People who really care.'

Another strong word.

'You've always done it, long as I've known you. You seem to need to see how far you can throw them. Lucky for you some of us are on strong elastic, so they don't go far. But you've got to break this pattern of behaviour, Porky.'

'I see. Any more, or is that all the homespun? And when's it my turn? When do I get to tell you what I think of you?'

'Any time you like,' Roderick said, getting up. 'Feel free. I know I let you down, once. Should have written more, tried to get to see you when we were courting. And when you sent me that letter I shouldn't have accepted it.'

'What, then?' I asked, a funny feeling in me, mention of this old stuff.

'Should have stopped you marrying – someone else, I suppose,' he said, reflecting. 'Should have come marching home, indignant like.'

Felt quite breathless, wondering if he was going to

162

say next still carrying a torch.

'I've never regretted marrying Amy, if that's your idea,' he said. 'Think. Can you see Amy throwing all these tantrums?'

'*Wait till she gets to my age*,' I said, and that hit home. He looked a bit thoughtful, then.

'You want to take more care,' he goes on, softer. 'Not go rushing off, taking jobs all over. Stan says you're in that Pizza Parlour now. Jack it in! You don't need the money.'

'Handy.'

'I know. But what's Dorelia's baby going to do if its grandmother's working all the time? And Dorelia's going to need you around, isn't she? It's her first.'

Something unnatural about a man who understands a woman's needs like that.

'I have to think on that one,' I said carefully.

'Do. I'll tell Stan he can come back now, shall I?'

And for some reason this infuriated me too.

'He'd better come and ask me that himself!' I cried. 'Not frightened of me, is he, for God's sake?'

When he'd gone I sat and waited for Stan to turn up. Had half suspected he'd been sat in Roderick's van outside. But the afternoon just wore on and on.

Made a pot of tea and then combed hair and applied lashings of *Passionate Cerise*, hoping to look wet-lipped and sultry like Joan Collins, though effect more as if just eaten whole pot blackcurrant jelly.

Sat and waited.

Nine o'clock.

Ten.

Won't come now. Probably in pub with *her*.

And Roderick, Amy, Wayne and Dorelia, all laughing and drinking, cracking jokes and having a good time.

Dragged up to bed. Couldn't be bothered to wash.

Only as eyes closing remembered had no tea.

163

*   *   *

Sunday, still no word. Toyed with idea of using telephone. Thought sod it.

Washed hair and read in bath, book about concentration camps and gas chambers and beefy women with whips who made lampshades out of babies' skins.

Wondered I ever dared to feel depressed.

Woke at half past five. Birds singing, lovely grey dawn breaking over South Norwood roofs.

Made tea, flipped on immersion for a bath. Stepped on scales.

Alleluia, praise de Lord, another four pounds gone. Still, nasty little voice insisting, Yeah, but what a way to lose it.

Applied White Satin with a heavy hand. Didn't feel like breakfast.

Sweeping under parlour palms with Jack and Trace smoking and giggling when Big Mick comes in, hungover. Early, because hasn't been home to bed.

His curly hair all anyhow, bags under eyes, designer stubble, the whole Bob Geldorf look. Attractive, if you like that kind of thing.

Trace and Jack stub out, pretend to stack cups in spires. Big Mick groans.

'Any aspirin on you, 'Reen?'

Nope. I offer to satchet out to early chemist and he's suitably grateful, saying been here all night, wasn't worf going home. Wishes he was dead.

Don't we all?

Out and back swiftly. Make him black coffee which he swallows with the aspirins and then nearly vomits as mixture hits the inflamed lining of his stomach.

But the beat goes on. Nothing stands in the path of the inexorable Pizza business or if it does, got suicide wish. Just hope our Mick gets paid for it.

164

'Don't you worry. I'll rip 'em off for every bit of overtime on their scabby timesheet and then some,' he tells me savagely.

Hates the buggers. Americans, I believe. *Provincials.* Well, colonials.

Out of work bums saunter in – Reeboks and frayed jeans. Trace and Jack flit between tables, biros poised.

'Sorry, can't 'elp yer!' when a kid wants coffee only.

What a dump this is. Carrying great stacks of cups where they've put them near the kitchen, when Trace comes stumbling past, white and holding her stomach with both hands.

'Bloody period,' she gasps, doubling up and settles for a smoke on steps by door leading to refrigerator yard. 'I don't care what he says, I'm not bloody going back in there till this eases off.'

Dicey, with Mick in the mood he is. I offer aspirin and black coffee – panseer all ills.

Then of course, he whirls in demanding to know what's up. Trace hurls cig. stub at fridges and faces him, obviously ill and in pain.

'Christ, this whole establishment's crumbling,' he says. 'Look, give 'Reen your bib. 'Reen, don't argue. Get out there. Loada shoppers just come in.'

Twelve o'bloody clock. Crucial crunch time, loopy lunch time. Out in front in bib and apron, no time to fix hair.

'Yes, madam, what can I get you?' (?Pizza with pepperoni, sliced salami, mozzarella, casalinga, oregano, peeled tomatoes, sprinkled basil or just Spam?)

'I'd like a coffee, please.'

'Sorry, madam, we don't do that on its own.'

'Is that so? Well, then I'll just visit The Coffee Shop. No extra purchase needed there.'

'Expensive, madam. Here you get a luscious, fresh, hot Pizza thrown in for the same price as two cups of coffee at The Coffee Shop.'

'Really? Not winding me up?'

'Why don't you try it and see?'

'Oh well, then, if you're really sure ...'

'Not bad,' says Big Mick, smiling for the first time since yesterday early morning. 'Good girl.'

Back and forth, back and forth and all that lovely washing up piling in kitchen. Soon no crockery clean enough for punters. Lady complains of lipstick not her own on cup. Mick loads machine. Trace washes a few cups under cold tap and wipes them hastily on rag used for surfaces. Unfortunately I'd wrung it out in bleach. Gives coffee no end of a distinctive tang. Mick loads some more. Trace uses cold tap. Got to keep the customers satisfied.

Then Trace goes home and Jackie comes out with period pains in sympathy. If I have to be even mildly pleasant just one more time I'll die.

'Right, that does it,' Mick says and hastening departure of some sturdy matrons with bogus promise of White Sale up Bentall's, turns the sign on the door.

CLOSED. Until six o'clock.

The rush had eased off about four, but even so someone comes up and hammers.

'Too sodding bad!' Mick calls out from the kitchen.

'Bit *naughty*, isn't it?' I asked.

'No one'll know unless you tell 'em,' he said. 'Help me with these plates, eh?'

Load after load goes into the machine. Finally place fit for fussy night shift worker, whoever she is.

'*Eileen*,' said Mick, and laid a finger against the side of his nose and winked.

Either he's having it off with her or there isn't such a person and he's fiddling her wage. Frankly, too tired to care.

'You deserve something nice,' Mick said.

'You, I suppose.'

'No, not me,' he said, taking me by the hand and suddenly pulling me along.

166

Thought he meant a cup of coffee then, and was about to say No thanks, I seen what goes in them perkers, when he led me to a door in back always kept locked and produced a key from a keyring on his belt.

Winked again and pushed open the door. Stairs there, wooden and dusty, steep, leading up and round. He gave me a gentle push.

'Ladies first.'

They led up into a high, arched room with rafters, long windows right down to the floor, with diamond panes. Dim light. Long trestle tables with stumps of candles in green bottle, everything covered in a film of dust. At one end a bar or counter piled with plastic fruit and festoons of drying hops.

He pulled up a little table by the bar and snapped his lighter at the candle. Lovely dull, intimate glow.

'What would madam prefer?' he asked.

'What you got?' And he whisked behind the bar and came out with a bottle of Chateau Neuf du Pape, light red and glittering in the glow.

I never tasted anything so nice. And it was tiddly-making, gave you a gorgeous glow just like the candle. We had one glass quite slow, relaxing, then another and another. And it all rolled down so smooth and quiet and delicious.

'Sorry no petit fours,' he said and we giggled.

Asked him where we were.

'Local gay palace,' he said. 'Where they come for pickups.'

'Won't they mind us drinking their wine?'

'Expect so if they knew.'

Well we finished off the bottle and he got another one, and made me laugh, doing a mincing act with a limp wrist, calling me duckie. And when we finished that bottle it was six, and time to get downstairs.

Eileen – she *was* real – come in just as he was locking up the gay bar door and she looked at me, not 'alf 'ard.

167

Shrivelled little thing, all bones. Wanted a word but I said good night tootsweet and hurried out.

'Blimey, you need tidy up,' I told *Semper Idem* when I got in. Did and all. Kitchen not too bad but 'Reeny's things all over lounge. And on the table a note for 'Reeny from her husband Stan.

Where are you? it said.

'*Semper Idem*,' I said, giggling.

'1, Kitchener Close, South Norwood, London, England, the World, the Universe . . .' Trailed off. Didn't know what came next. Anyway, surely he knew where I was. Must have done to have left the note. Silly.

'*Came round five thirty see if you wanted come for a drink tonight*', the note went on. An olive branch, if ever I saw one. Point was, did I want it?

'Already had a drink,' I whispered, and let the note flutter to the floor.

Didn't feel like food.

Tidied, then crashed out in bed about nine thirty and almost slept through alarm, though not quite.

Mick looking as though he hadn't slept again. Eyes all bloodshot. Insisted I waitress. Too good for washing up, he said. Kept fairly close to me all day as if about to say something. But busy and probably changed his mind.

Got on scales. Have lost 21 lbs. unless scales liars.

They're not.

Old jeans once thought so great all baggy on me now.

Pay day and Mick with little brown envelopes. Kept mine till last.

'Doing anything tonight?' he asked all casual as he dished out.

'Gay bar again?' I asked hopefully, giving him saucy smile.

'Ssh!' he said, glancing round. 'My night off. Tomorrow,

168

too. Not that that matters,' he said hastily, as if he'd suddenly thought I'd think he was asking to spend the night. 'Just had the idea – a drink somewhere quietly, to discuss your promotion.'

'If Chateau Neuf du Pape again,' I told him lightly while the lovely word 'promotion' rolled and echoed round my head.

'Ah! Can't promise that,' he said and smiled. Dead attractive with his stubble gone.

At four he signalled me *That's it*. Went and took apron off and pansied up. Used lots of White Satin because my rule is, if a little is good, then more must be a whole lot better. Just as was leaving, turned back to look at myself in glass.

Didn't look like good old 'Reen at all. Or perhaps there was a bit of her, but much *more* like 'Reeny Purkiss as was, thirty year ago.

No, can't be, I thought and lingered. But it was. It's the round cheeks that do it . . . no, the *weight*. Say rather, loss of. And all these years I been carrying round that ageing, surplus tissue. No wonder S. had hankering for the train shop girl.

Think about him later, eh? Just now I satcheted off with Mick.

Strange to be out with a man who was taller than me. Mostly when shopping or visiting the pub I look down on to Stanley Spink's shiny bits.

This was rather nice. Made me feel really small and sort of fragile.

Went to a Turkish place in Spring Lane.

Excited by smell of food. Not eaten properly for days.

'You're really something, you know that?' Mick murmured after a little dark-haired waiter had brought wine.

Offered me a cigarette. That was Turkish too.

Tables small with crumpled, red-checked cloths, socking great muriels on walls, all garish colours. Breathing in harsh tobacco fumes and secretly wishing had painted nails to match.

'Yes, indeed,' he went on. 'But why, oh why do you cut your hair? With that lovely blonde colour you should wear it full and free like a lion's mane.'

I'd always thought that as you got older you should wear it shorter.

'Noway. That way you'd end up bald,' he said definitely. 'That sort of talk just makes me mad. Why, for heaven's sake?'

I murmured something about suitable for older women.

'Balls!' he said. 'Excuse me.'

The little waiter had poured the wine, a rough old plonk called Piz, hee hee, made you wince on its own but went down a treat with Shish Kebab.

'Attractive woman is attractive woman is attractive woman,' Mick said, explaining and I smiled at him, mouth fulla lamb and onions. Made mental note to grow hair.

'That's right,' he said, smiling back. 'No good going round with a face like a John Dory.'

Laughed, and when waiter came back and said sorry, couldn't manage another Piz, only Buzbag in the house, laughed some more.

Had a good time.

Later he dropped me off at home and I waltzled in full of it all, ready to tell Stan.

And of course he wasn't there, only empty house with unmade bed and curtains still drawn from this morning. Neighbours must have thought there'd been a death.

Weighed self. 8 st. 3 lbs. Even after heavy meal with wine. Jubilant. Slim for first time in years. Went downstairs to kitchen to see what I could find to eat.

*　　*　　*

Saturday

He phoned in morning, also flowers from Mick.

Wanted to come round 'to talk'. I said alright and got busy arranging Mick's flowers in vases all over the place. Couldn't help but catch the eye.

He came. Said, 'You got admirer, then?'

Perhaps.

Then – 'Blimey, what you done to yourself? *No tits!*'

Annoyed. *My* business.

'What you done?' he said. 'Where they gone?'

'Nowhere,' I told him coldly. 'They're just where they've always been.' But I peeked down the top of my sweater to make sure. Bit unnerving, him saying things like that.

'Oh dear,' he said. 'I know what it is, you've gone and slimmed.'

'I assure you I haven't done it special,' I said.

'I suppose *he* likes you like that?'

'Maybe.'

'Well I don't. I like something you can get 'old of.'

'Too bad. You left home, remember?'

'You threw me out, you mean.'

Verge of rowing. Fortunately Miss Sweetbush from the library rang just then to say Georgette Heyer reprint in, three new Mills and Boon and new Romance imprint from large publisher on label of *Roses, Roses.*

Told her that was chocolates or Labour Party, ho, ho, but would she save them anyway. Then stood and wondered why the hell I wanted books about Romance. Rang her back, said start reserving cookery books, esp. Turkish ones, and she astonished.

So was he.

Said what wrong with English and coming up the pub? I said, 'Up the pub, up the pub. All you think about.'

'No it's not,' he said and then, hastily – 'I just want to be with you, 'Reen.'

'Ha! Funny way of showing it.'

171

'You coming, then?'

'No,' I told him. 'Washing my hair tonight.'

He all miserable.

Come to think of it, that was excuse I give him thirty year ago when courting and I had my period. Laughed like drain when realized.

Later bending to touch toes and massage scalp so blood gets to roots of hair. Remembered reading somewhere that makes it grow faster.

Lonely in evening. Phone went and rushed to answer it hoping Mick but only cold sell Double Glazing. Told salesman to put windows up own arse. Felt better.

Washed hair. A millimetre longer.

Played old Buddy Holly tapes but unaccountably began to cry so put King Elvis on instead. Better but not much.

Lost all desire to pig on food. Went to bed at eight after baked beans on slimming bread. Sodding miserable.

D. came round Sunday morning. Very, very glad to see her.

Wanted to know if I'd have her daddy back and I said lightly, 'course I would, only a tiny tiff.

'He doesn't seem to think so.'

'Dorelia,' I said, 'when you get to my age you sometimes go off half cock.' And then stopped and laughed, because it sounded funny. I mean, I always been off half cock, anybody would.

She looked at me peculiar.

'You sometimes say more than you mean,' I told her. 'Like in adolescence.'

'Overreact?'

'Yes.'

'The Change?'

'The Change.'

'Poor Mummy. But if Daddy comes round you'll be nice to him?'

172

'Don't you worry, sweetheart,' I told her. 'We'll sort something out.'

Wondered if Jackie and Trace would resent me doing tables, but no. New girl, school-leaver, for washing up.

Trace said, 'About time we had help,' and Jackie added, 'I see it coming from the first.'

'What?'

'Him. He look at you that way right from Day One. Mind, I wouldn't say no meself if he asked me nicely.'

'Didn't know you was into wrinklies, Jack,' Trace said, and fell about.

Did wonders for my moral. Jackie said, 'No offence, 'Reen, enjoy it while you still can.' And Trace said, 'Look out, here comes Grandad,' and they scarpered.

Mick come up and asked what that about.

'Girls,' I told him. He sighed.

'Got three of my own.'

Oh? That rather took the shine off things a bit.

'How old?' I asked, and he said, 'Fourteen, sixteen, eighteen.'

Somebody Family Planned.

'I'm separated,' he added, watching me. 'Smart money says I'll be divorced by the end of the year.'

Day off in lieu Thursday this week.

Work all a go go, and pleased – very, very, very pleased with new figure, even if Stanley ain't. Also wage packet coming Friday that is mine all mine. Shan't jack it in, our Roderick.

Wednesday morning Mick says all right for a drink this evening if you knock off one, back four-five, work for an hour, but pay as usual?

Agree. Excited, though part oddly depressed, though never in same way as before. Have climbed right up out of deep dark well, totally wivout aid mighty Vitamin B complex.

173

No. This sadness more like little warning voice. Must just be old conditioning, though, 'cos this nice girl is going to, tonight.

Then panic. Home at one fifteen, rushed up to bathroom cabinet where ancient medical supplies. Have new packet Featherlites in bag, but when serving one *pizza olio e pomodoro* had nasty sudden thought; *don't know him. What if he won't put one on?*

Dutch cap in small plastic snap-to case. Hold cap up to window light and inspect for holes.

Remember with pang how refused to go on using it with S. Too messy, put me right off, I said. But that wasn't the real reason.

Remember also how he complained wearing rubbers like paddling with thick socks. Hardened resolve. He should know all about wearing socks.

Rushed out, back to shops and bought handy tube of Orthogynol, then bathed, applied all, washed hair, dried upsidedown and so fluffed out. New earrings. Stood in front of mirror to admire effect of naked body then aghast with dismay as that stupid, melodramatic author Aurora North-Brightley would put it.

Not a single-bingle, sodding thing to wear.

All outfits hopelessy bloody fuddy duddy, duddy duddy *fat.*

Sat on bed and looked at watch.

Out to shops again (dressed first), this time Miss Selfridge, Richard's, Next. *Beautiful* floral top and flowing skirt. (Also skinny jeans, three little tops and three new bras and pairs of panties. Don't want tits rattling round like loose peas in a pod, do we?)

White Satin, then out again, free, hair blowing in wind.

Simply couldn't remember the last time I felt this way. Years rolled back like huge unwanted carpet. Wolf whistle in street. Happy, happy, happy, immense bouquet of flowers to Joan Collins, any others who helped roll the carpet back.

174

Why did I let Time drag me down so sodding long? Am sexy randy little bitch on heat, flashing long, painted nails, swinging bag.

('Swinging old bag?' says little voice. Be quiet, shut up, sit down, fade out and otherwise *scram*. Had 'nough of you already.)

Just got to Piggi's, pushing door and reflecting on unfairness; S.S. simply didn't appreciate *real me*, when tears spring up. Dash them away with back of manicured hand. Damn him. I don't love Spink.

Tears intensify the blue of eyes. Trace does double take. 'Get you!'

Don Piggi clothes in back. Whistle from Mick. Comes up, puts hands round waist and instant fire leaps from hands to groin (mine).

'Oh, 'Reeny, 'Reeny,' he murmurs, burying his face in my neck. 'You smell so delicious I could eat you.'

Later, later.

Half wonder if he'll close the shop while we . . . but no. At six he takes his jacket from the stand behind the parlour palm and nods towards the gay, gay bar upstairs. But won't there be people up there?

It's empty, though chairs set out and dusted. So will it be Chateau Neuf du Pape as usual? Indeed. Slides down smooth as Castrol GTX, though yummier. More, more.

The little voice pipes up to say don't think we could face what coming next without it, eh, eh?

Down, girl.

He's holding my hand now, electricity in arc between us. Haven't *ached* like this for years and bloody years.

'No more talk,' he says quietly and stands up, still holding my hand and leads me over to yet another door.

This bit straight out Aurora, I think thrillingly.

Room with a settee, so bald, so naked in the centre there, impossible mistake for anything but what it is. And so . . . this must be where gays will bring their pickups.

Must have seen my face.

'They don't *all* do it standing up, you know,' he says, trying effect of feeble joke.

'Never really thought.'

True. Beyond Stan's saying, 'Blimey, better stand with me back to the wall in here,' when we blundered into funny pub in Chelsea once, don't know so much about them.

Settee cover tatty, splattered with stiff – and to my eyes, *still* stiffening stains.

Emotion drains away quicker'n hot piddle in the snow.

'You have to be joking!' I say, pointing to yukky thing.

He looks at it, back at me, then at it again and nods reluctantly, and sighs.

'Perhaps you're right.' And leads the way back again, no doubt for more Chateau Neuf.

Barperson arrives, looking like Brenda from The Gates only less butch. Nods cheerfully at Mick, who smiles, the way a girl would with a man.

And little voice inside says, '*Look*.'

'Swinging the other way tonight then, are we?' says the cheery one.

Mick frowns. 'Lend us your keys.'

'Car keys or flat keys, sweetie?'

'Both.'

'Look, dear,' barperson says. 'I know I owe you one, but . . .'

'*One*?' Mick says heavily.

'Oh, alright,' says Cheerful, a bit sulky, but by this time Ms Spink is heading for the stairs. One hell of awful, slow, middle-aged fool, but clean. And likely to remain so.

Trace and Jack smoking in cleared place below and CLOSED sign on door 'till seven. Look at me, then at each other. Say nothing.

Breast (what left of it) heaving. Oh God, they *knew*.

'Tata, chaps,' I says. 'See you Friday.'

'Wouldn't bet on it,' says Trace.

176

Outside in cold again. Story of my life.

And all dressed up and nowhere to go.

Only one place *to* go. Home.

Back at *Semper Idem* bathed again and rewashed hair. No note from S. this time. Sat watching the TV unseeing, forming plan.

What beats me is why those kids didn't warn me. But probably thought old enough to look out for self.

Oh yeah.

Thursday

Up seedy cafe, Lewisham way, in rain, twelve o'clock. Daffodils in window boxes browning at edges as if burnt. Already first, bright green of hawthorn deepening.

Love spring. Usually. Not today. Not today when on way to Kay's Pantry, well-known haunt of gormands. You know, the one where the pepper and salt pot holes get all bunged up with . . . That's the one.

Thought better order something. Got scabby scrambled egg on toast, looked like cat's puke. Only pretended eat it, very slow. Plastic bag underneath table all the time.

Think at first out on fool's errand, but round about one o'clock, in she comes and seems for dreadful, sick-making moment, all alone. Then her mates trail in after her, punk hair blazing. One pink, one orange.

She looked over and didn't recognize me at first. Then did double take like Trace. Even then not really sure because fat – or losing it – alters face so. You look like someone who reminds them of you, it could *be* you, only much thinner. And it is you, only much thinner.

They sit down and order and on off-chance, I suppose, that it's me, she starts.

Laughing a lot by time iced buns and orangeade come up. Me motherly at first, watching them. (Surprised.)

Want to tell them don't eat that rubbish, need vitamins, minerals, eat up your greens, finish all your milk. You eaten up your crusts? Then you can get down.

But I remember.

Never a look across at me. But louder still, laughing round the corner of iced bun. She got 'ooked nose like Barbra Streisand. And that *frizzy* hair.

Talking dirty now. Saying how catch herpes, crabs, all kindsa lice.

Like you, you little lowlife. Set up book against encrusted cruet set, pretend to read.

She cackles louder than before, telling how someone drove her home last night from somewhere. How she asked him in for bit more than coffee and a drink.

And where was her mum at that time, in bed and fast asleep? maternal bit wondered. But turns out she's living in one room, one of those contravertibles, toilet and wash hand basin tucked away behind folding screen. Bedsits, we used to call them in the old days.

Well, she told us what she done with him, straight forward enough, nothing kinky. Loadsa laughs over size of bloke's whatsit, couldn't be Stan.

You'd never do it, I thought, if you knew the way young girls can take the mickey afterwards. Hate it, hate it, hate it, to be a man and find out they're laughing over size of what you prize the most. Know of one young nurse who peered, then said, 'That it? It can't be. Seen better than that on mortuary slab last night.'

And all that retailing the faking and the filth. Never mind the Countess winning Oscars, this one supreme award for acting and no messing. For after taking last night and his dong apart and still not looking over here she starts again. I'm sicky now and push that blasted egg away from me, bringing waitress out, so have to pretend to eat again, and read. Perhaps I should have Oscar, 'n all.

Don't want to listen about Stan and yet I do.

'Cuntstruck like all the rest,' young madam laughs, and this time, yes, her sly eyes come round and she's squinting at me from the corners. I kept looking at page apparently, raising forkful of yellow muck towards my mouth.

'Practically implored me. Got right down and kissed it. Peeled me clothes all serious like in church.'

Yes, that was Stanley. Serious, like in church – though what would she know about church? But him wanting a certain thing so bad it was positively worship – that was him. That's when I knew she seen me and was doing it on purpose.

'Did 'e sing 'ymn?' little Pink Girl asked with giggles.

'Did 'e wear socks?' I heard myself say, getting up.

Gasp of absolute, achieving pleasure from Miss Madam. Done it. Got old trout rising nicely.

'Who you?' she says, settling back all cool in chair. Enjoying this. Greasy denim jacket flops open. She got chest, a good one. And knows it. And thin fleshy legs.

That too confirms it was my Stanley that she meant.

'Said "Did he wear socks?" ' I told her, so much fury in me I can't hardly control.

'What's it to you?' she says, spluttering with half-laughter. Too funny, this old trout, to be treated seriously. Glances at mates, inviting them to share this.

Don't know that they knew what was going on. Pink just looked embarrassed, Orange gawping so wide, might catch flies. Well, you don't usually get stranger in teashop asking if last night's lover wearing socks.

'Who is this old bat?' Orange asked and Sharon said never seen me in her life before.

Pink giggled nervously, all high and shrill and the waitress came out and started to hover near.

'You been with my Stan,' I said to Sharon.

'Never,' she said, all flip. 'Who's Stan?'

'My husband.'

'Oh, your husband.'

179

'You remember. Or have you had so many you can't think?'

'You calling me a whore?' cries Sharon, not entirely laid back now. What perception.

Waitress gets all agitated. No one takes blind bit of notice.

'Well aren't you?' I said to Sharon.

'No! You mind your own business, fucking slag!'

Orange said to me deliberate, 'Why don't you just go away?'

'Go away?' I asked, puzzled. Couldn't see the sense of that. Red (yes, it really is red) rage coming behind the eyes. Reached out and grabbed a handful of long, frizzy hair.

She screeched. My God, did she howl. Waitress come running up. Pink and Orange shouted out. By then I had 'orrible stuff wound tightly round the knuckles of one hand.

Gave an enormous pull.

'Ow!' yelled that bitchy little thing. 'Ow, ow, ow!'

Good. Tugged again hard as I could and felt something come away in my hand. Felt it tear. *Nasty.*

'Please! Please stop,' the waitress gasped and put her hands feebly on top of mine. Pink turned and ran out sharpish, then, all chicken suddenly. Don't think she'll be in the gang again. But Orange held on to me, grinning; had an idea she enjoying our little scrap.

'Have to call the police!' the waitress cried.

'Do,' I told her. 'Probably close you down. You ain't displaying menu prices, that's offence. If *Health* people don't get you first.' Waved at the spotted-brown tablecloths, the fly-blown walls. 'You could catch death in here.'

She stood all helpless and whimpering and Sharon come upright, mascara in black streaks on her face. But Orange turns and looks at me, her eyes in slits.

I seen eyes like that before. Larch Mulliner's.

'Fuck *off*,' she says, deliberate again.

I went. Oh, I went. Heart like metronome, tick-tick, tick-

180

tick. But happy. Yes, happy. That's what life all about, innit, wisps of frizzy hair caught in the ring Mum left me, the one I wear on my right hand.

Only regret is not six foot tall and built like Sean Connery in *Goldfinger*, then I'd have really shown her.

Hummed as I tripped back down Whitefoot Lane.

That screeching little cow will have a bald patch for some time.

About three this morning woke up tired and aching. Suppose the bitch brings charges for assault? Couldn't sleep after that.

And then saw very clearly little louse been acting. She wanted me to think the worst. *He'd been telling me the truth.*

And oh God, I'd thrown him out.

Up very early and down road to Piggi's. Pay Day.

Doors shut and bolted. No sign of our Mick. Trace came at last and stuck her head out.

'You,' she said. 'Well, thanks for bloody nothing.'

'Eh?'

'He said to give you double wages and week's notice.'

Handed me a packet and a note.

Sacked.

'Don't bother coming in,' she says.

I shrugged. Got me wages. Turned to go.

'I seen you!' she yells after me. 'You couldn't keep your bloody hands off him!'

Shrugged again. Got wages, like I said.

Anyone would think I was 'pickpocket, hear her talk.

Went home, stopping to buy packet *Love My Hair*, Honey Blonde shade, also curlers, grips, large Ozone-happy moose and sharp, sharp pair of styling scissors.

Cleaned house, did nets, then hair. By eleven, pilesa fragrance, all neatly folded, also short-haired, buttercup

181

'Reen, but no sign of Stanley. Then remembered today Friday. Still at work.

Rang Dorelia and said all misunderstanding between parents over now and I was going to have her daddy back. She glad.

About twelve Amy called to say Eamonn shacked up with funny girl from The Feathers, where dreadful Black Brian hangs out, a gin-swilling Irish girl who keeps kitchen so you stick to surfaces in there. I said hope they'll be very happy and she spoke sharpish back, our Amy.

Still, not standing for any old nonsense from her.

'Tell Stan his tea'll be ready at six,' I told her.

'You don't understand, do you?' she said.

'I don't?'

'No. You've graciously decided you want him back after all, but it isn't quite like that.'

'It isn't?'

'You can't just expect him to come running.'

'I can't?'

' 'Reeny,' she said, almost losing her temper (for Amy). 'He's not going to come back just like that just because you say so.'

'Why ever not?' I asked, really wanting to know. After all, it's me that's doing the forgiving; for a bit. And maybe I got to admit openly I was wrong about Sharon Trainshop, enough for anyone. (But if I was, still glad I pulled her hair; can take it done on behalf of other wives she's wronged.)

' 'Reen,' Amy says slowly. 'Stan's feelings have been very badly hurt. You wouldn't believe him when he told you the truth.'

'We don't know yet he was telling me the truth.'

'Oh, for crying out loud!' Amy said, most unlike her. 'Don't you know him after thirty years?'

I don't know.

What do know is I miss him and I want to talk.

Told about Thursday in Kay's Pantry and thought heard smothered laugh.

'Not funny, for God's sake!' I shouted.

'Wasn't laughing,' she said, bloody liar. 'But surely this makes things clearer. For it comes down to this, 'Reeny – whose word are you prepared to take, his or that of a play-acting, malicious little slut?'

'Well, think on,' she said, then changing subject, 'Sorry you lost your job.'

'Who told you?'

'Dorelia. Also seems to be under impression you want Stanley back whatever. She was really happy about that. She believes in him, you see.'

Everyone does, it seems. And how can the Family be wrong?

'Amy,' I said, facing the now unthinkable, and like her speaking slowly, 'if Stan don't want to come back, what'll I do?' And I waited for her to weigh in with the comforting advice, how to play it, what to say, also her reassurance she'd do her bit, talking to Stan.

'You got *Semper Idem*,' she says shortly, just a touch of something in her voice. Iron. Then she rang off.

Well, I was astounded. Amy doesn't speak to me like that. But honesty compels me to admit that yes, she bloody did. *Did*. The once. Not usual.

Amy changing too? Remembered something Roderick said about me pushing people away. Sat down suddenly to think this one out. Oh God, not Amy too.

Couldn't think why this should be so dreadful, Amy pushed away. I mean she's irritating with her soft voice and her religion and (sometimes) being right and . . .

. . . always there.

Nothing really worf a monkey's if she's not.

And Stanley. Oh God, that's what it's all about.

Only *Semper Idem* when he's there.

Well, for starters, who's going to cut the bloody hedge? Would give anything to hear him whistling *Balls to Mr Bangelstein* right now while fetching Black 'n' Decker.

183

Got shears and went out into road and started on hedge, looking out towards main road occasionally hoping he'd happen along and see poor little woman valiantly trying to cope with a man's tasks. (Can reach top easily, he has to stand on box.)

Did it nice, if tilted a bit towards Thames, then saw nosy neighbours peering out behind curtains. Thought they might wonder where he gone, also might form own conclusions, like detained somewhere awaiting Her Majesty's pleasure.

Left hedge unfinished, went indoors.

Early night.

Seven o'clock (a.m.) called Amy once again.

'You'll have to talk to him about it,' she said. Sounded a bit weary.

'Talk? He ain't into talking,' I told her. 'He don't fancy thrashing things out. *He's* not a New Man.'

'Never mind the labels!' she said sharply. 'You want him back, don't you? Then be nice to him.'

'Be what?'

'Nice.'

'You mean old fashioned?'

' 'Reeny,' Amy says heavily, 'does that matter now? Forget the jargon. Go for the man.'

'Man? Man? Oh, you mean Stanley.'

'Pay attention. Doesn't it strike you the Feminist Statement is already very old? You need to move beyond it now. Particularly with Stan.'

'Where is he, then?' I asked, annoyed.

'Got early train to Petts Wood,' she said, hanging up.

Petts Wood. And got early train. This can only mean one thing, olive branch. Biggest and best olive branch I ever seen.

He'd gone to look for houses in Petts Wood.

Felt really chipper. Pansied up, then caught train to Victoria, tube Charing Cross, then down train. Had plenty of time reflect how nice he being. Probably there already, wandering tree-lined streets. Planned what I would say when we met up. Not a lot, just enough to let him know welcome back.

Petts Wood in white letters, plain green sign. Only two platforms and a siding, poplar trees, backside of shops, a square with taxis and a pub.

Surprisingly I come on him straight away. Draped over little footbridge at top of steps, looking both ways at once like god of the New Year, London and Dover. Didn't see me till I touched his arm.

A bit startled. 'What you doing here?' Then gazed back towards London once again. And a thrill ran through me as I realized he hadn't wanted to be discovered. This house business meant as a surprise.

'Looks good, eh?' I told him.

'Certainly does.'

'You must be very keen.'

'You know I am.' He almost turned to face me for an instant. 'Never gave you cause to doubt it, did I?'

'There *was* a time,' I admitted. 'Happy as elephant up a tree, you said.'

'I said that?' He sounded genuinely astonished. 'Never. I was always enthusiast. You gimme books about it, Christmas.'

Down below a line of boxy carriages swung round the slow curve of the London bend and chuntered underneath us through the station. Didn't stop. Looked as if more important things on mind.

'202 Class 6L DEMU, no. 1011 84,' he murmured. 'Strange. Thought *they'd* all been withdrawn. Can't have, I suppose. Wonder if there'll be a route learning car through here at all?'

'Anyone would think,' I said through gritted teeth, 'You come out here just to look at trains.'

'Well I didn't come for the fresh air,' he said. 'What did you think? This is a handy little bridge. Imagine,

185

the Golden Arrow used to pass through here!'

Yeah, imagine.

'You didn't come to look at houses, then?'

'You know, I was down 'ere once,' he said, smiling fondly, remembering. 'And she stopped. Just stopped. *There.*' He pointed. 'Sat there, steaming, chuf-chuff, chuf-chuff, you know? I ran up and down, I remember, looking at her first this side of the bridge, then the other and a little kid train spotting, *he* ran up and down shouting, "It's stopped! The Golden Arrow's stopped!" ' He smiled again. 'Because of course, she didn't, not before Dover, well, maybe Orpington sometimes . . .'

Be nice, be nice. But oh, the effort, mother.

'Bit early, but fancy a drink?' I said instead of hitting him.

'If you like.'

'Sort of celebrate us together again.'

'Well as to that, 'Reen, as to that . . .'

Went in The Daylight Inn. Not as nice inside as I expected. Trust Amy.

Sank a few jars. Had jumbo sausage and french bread but they forgot the mustard.

Not a word between us about coming back, or anyone sorry for their base suspicions. Not even *won't do that again*. Most things, I mean the great important things are better left unsaid. Still, understood.

All over, anyway, that bitter time of splitting up and accusations. Amy was right. I been a bloody fool.

And, of course, he just come here for the trains. Don't matter.

'Least you knew where to find me,' he said, munching crisps.

'Still fancy East Anglia,' he says later. 'Whatever we decide to do in future. All those generations, buried in country churchyards, father, son . . .'

'Mother, daughter . . .'

'Continuous, like.'

186

'Some would of got killed off in wars they made.'

'Politicians, rich people make wars. Poor people get conscripted.'

'And think they're doing it for King and country,' I said, remembering Grandad. Still haven't fixed those bayonets.

'Poor people just want to be let alone. Not vote Tory, not really join anything, just leave be.'

Nearest time we ever got to talking.

'You still going to keep allotment?' I asked.

'You guessed it,' he said. 'What about you? I mean, what do you want?'

'Just you,' I told him and watched embarrassed look come on his face. 'And Dorelia,' I added.

'Couldn't expect her to move to a country district,' he said, drawing patterns in some beer spill with his finger.

'Don't do that! Now, no villages,' I went on to warn him, case he was getting ideas. 'No places with just little shops sell dog food, soap and stamps and that's your lot.'

'I wasn't thinking of it,' he said, looking straight at me. ' 'Reen . . . Something we must have out.'

'Your plonker,' I says, happiness and Daylight lemonade going to my head just a bit.

'Be serious.'

'Can't. It's my Celtic blood.'

'Thought you was Cockney.'

'Anglo-Saxon,' I told him. 'Look at my yellow hair.'

'And getting yellower with age,' he says. Then after a pause, 'Ain't we all?'

Coloured couple went past us then, laughing and holding hands, looking for place to sit. Suddenly I envied them their laughter.

'Must be funny knowing exactly what colour hair your kids are going to have,' I said slowly, following them with my eyes. 'I mean, our lot, we don't know, we can't. Here's you, darkish – well, *was* – me fair, both with blue eyes, and there's Dorelia and Wayne . . .'

187

'Yes,' says Stan heavily, with feeling.

Sat thinking, both, about Brian at The Feathers with the dark, dark hair.

Soon after that home pretty toot damn sweet to South Norwood, largely because I went off Petts Wood there and then. In train, it wasn't so much a place, I discovered, as idea I'd had in mind, idea of gentle domesticity. And I'd had that under my hand all the time and had been busy overlooking it, the fool. Still, things seemed to be on the up. He appeared to be glad to be coming back.

Like they say on school reports, 'Reeny must try harder next time.

Oh, I *will!*

Mulliners met us corner of Kitchener Close.

'You surely want to hear about the kitten now,' they said, prancing up.

'Oh certainly,' I said. (Polite.)

'Well, dear Mr Thomson says,' they began, enjoying audience, 'that it's eating when he puts out scraps.'

'Terrific,' I said.

'Feeding quite well, but totally unable to fend for itself.'

'Lazy?'

'*Blind*. And it's a tortoiseshell, with tabby bits, a little queen. *Could* it be yours, we wondered?'

Don't care if it isn't. Having that.

'Sure to be,' I told them. 'That is, it certainly sounds like it. Would Mr Thomson ... ?'

'Quite possibly.'

Stood staring at them then, not seeing, thinking get kitten, no tea prepared, pick up Moussaka, stuffed Vine Leaves to go down Popo's, and then phone began ringing inside. Mulliners moved on smiling, to do good somewhere else.

And it was Wayne on the telephone saying Dorelia in labour and had been four hours, trying to reach me all morning.

*   *   *

So here we are in this waiting room smells of stale cig.
smoke and old antiseptic. Dirty, curling magazines
around, worn stacking chairs, upholstery bursting.

Wayne has promised us a champagne supper later.

I said to Stanley, 'Poor Baby. She won't be getting any
tonight.'

He looked scandalized.

'Meant the champagne,' I said. 'You got one-track
mind.'

'I didn't fancy it again until about five months,' I went
on, reminissing. 'I remember. Or was it six?'

He looked embarrassed again and opened his mouth
as if to say something then closed it again, then said,
'Yeah. She'll be crazy for a cup of tea.'

How high the ceilings are in these old dumps.

He said, 'What you writing, then?'

I told him, 'Shopping list.'

' 'Reen,' he said then.

'Yes?'

Everything's turning out all right. She'll have 'ealthy
child, and with any luck I can get him off this East Anglia
idea. With Baby's baby running around, shouldn't be too
hard.

Yes, life coming right side up again. Fast.

' 'Reen . . .'

I'll be able to push her out in her pram, and later she
can help me make a cake. Whoops, remember there's to
be no stereo gendering. Well she can help him up the
allotment. And to think foolish Granny nearly threw
Grandpa out. Well, that's one story that I won't be telling her.

'Snowmen in winter, sandcastles in summer,' I said to
him, smiling and nodding happily. He nodded back, but
looking worried. But everything's going to be all right
. . . long as Little Baby don't have blue-black hair.

*   *   *

7.40 p.m. He gone to Friends' Canteen for sandwiches and coffee. D. bin in labour now eight hours. Went in to see her once or twice but she really only wants Wayne. Feel supernuminous. We'd be better off at home with packet of Vine Leaves to go.

7.45 p.m. That's the time he comes in smelling of whisky and I say, 'You found a bar?' and he says, 'Mog, I tried holding it in and I can't no more, all this tension working in me so I feel I'll burst. I'm sorry, but maybe better to have this thing out right now while waiting so you don't get any more ideas about me coming back and don't go in to D. filling her with all false notions and things. I haven't been straight with you, Moggy, not one little bit. I gotta confess I lied to you, lied all along . . .'

And then that young nurse runs in at the double with a white face she tries to control and can't and says hurry extra quick to us, it's Dorelia.

And I don't know why.